D0143612

MOONLIGHT WEEPS

ALSO BY VINCENT ZANDRI

The Dick Moonlight P.I. Mystery Series
Moonlight Falls
Moonlight Mafia
Moonlight Rises
Blue Moonlight
Full Moonlight
Murder by Moonlight
Moonlight Sonata

The Jack Marconi Mystery Series
The Innocent
Godchild
The Guilty

The Chase Baker Thriller Series
The Shroud Key
Chase Baker and the Golden Condor

The Stand-Alones
The Remains
Scream Catcher
Lost Grace
The Concrete Pearl
Permanence
Everything Burns

The Shorts
Pathological
Banal
True Stories

VINCENT ZANDRI

MOONLIGHT WEEPS

A Dick Moonlight P.I. Mystery

Copyright 2014 by Vincent Zandri

First Edition: September 2014

All rights reserved. No part of the book may be reproduced in any
form or by any electronic or mechanical means, including
information storage and retrieval systems, without permission in
writing from the publisher, except by a reviewer who may quote brief
passages in a review.

Down & Out Books
3959 Van Dyke Rd, Ste. 265
Lutz, FL 33558
www.DownAndOutBooks.com

The characters and events in this book are fictitious. Any similarity to
real persons, living or dead, is coincidental and not intended by the
author.

The author is represented by MacGregor Literary, Inc.

Cover art and design by JT Lindroos

ISBN: 1-937495-74-4

ISBN-13: 978-1-937495-74-9

For Laura

"Sad thing is, you can still love someone
and be wrong for them."
—*Elvis Presley*

"Go ahead! I take your fucking bullets! You think
you kill me with bullets? I take your fucking
bullets! Go ahead!"
—*Tony Montana, Scarface*

Chapter 1

According to my schedule, I'm to meet Roland Hills, a.k.a. Elvis Presley, at the coffee shop in North Albany at eight in the morning. I would have met him at seven but, like the great Hound Dog in the sky, he's been hitting the booze a little too hard as of late. So, like a good employee, I let him sleep in.

That's me—Moonlight the teddy bear.

Pulling into a parking lot overcrowded with pickup trucks and cars, including an eighteen- wheeler parked diagonally, I find Hills' old Honda motorcycle and glide up beside it. I'm just about to get out and head inside to grab a coffee when I spot the big, black-haired, forty-something Elvis impersonator coming toward me, gripping two very large coffees. Electronically thumbing down the passenger side window on Dad's old 1978 hearse, I lean over the empty seat, ask him to get in.

He stops, shoots me a bulging-eye look, like he's seen his own ghost.

"Moonlight, I ain't gettin inside that thing."

Like his 1977 Fat Elvis beer gut, his Oklahoma accent sticks out like a sore thumb in Albany, New York. It's a cool May morning, but he's only got on a T-shirt, the words "Your Momma Lied" in big black letters expanding and distorting over his bloated belly.

"What's to be afraid of? It's not like sitting inside a hearse is gonna kill *you*, Elvis. Kinda works the other way around."

"You ain't hung-over like I am." His hands shake so badly the coffee is spilling out the little sippy holes

1

punched into the plastic lids. "I'm already near death."

"Just get in. The stuff I have to show you is better revealed in private."

"What stuff?"

"The stuff you're paying me to find out about your girlfriend."

He just stands there, his thick black hair and pork chop sideburns looking pasted onto his round face, his big gut hanging off his belt, hands shaking, coffee spilling.

"It's bad, ain't it?" His south-of-the-border twang raises an octave. Like he's about to cry. "Think I'm gonna be sick."

"If you're about to be sick, Elvis, blow your chunks in the lot. But hand me my coffee first."

"I'm okay." A beat passes. "Just not used to the love of my life cheating on me, is all."

"Guess now you know how her husband and your wife must feel."

He attempts to smile at that. But apparently he can't work up the strength. Reaching across the seat, I open the door for him. He gets in, stinking of old booze.

I take my coffee in hand and, at the same time, catch my reflection in the rearview mirror. I haven't been sleeping so great lately, what with being single and therefore free to roam the gin mills of my choice at all hours of the night. Worse, I've got a bank account that is so below zero it brain-freezes me even to think of it. Peering into my own brown eyes I spot a round face that needed a shave five days ago, and a head of hair so short you can see the scars crisscrossing my scalp like a road map—including the small dime-sized scar beside my right earlobe where, once upon a time, a piece of .22 caliber hollow-point bullet penetrated my skull. Standing up the collar on my leather coat with my free hand, I look away from the mirror, musing over my worn combat boots and dark, beat-up Levi's.

Suddenly, I smell something bad.

"Christ, Elvis, when was the last time you showered?"

"Been sleeping at the phone company." Elvis's day job consists of fixing broken computers at the local Verizon. "Ain't got no where's to go." He tries to sip his coffee, but his hand is trembling too much and most of it lands on his chin. Reaching into the side pocket on his baggy blue jeans, he withdraws a small bottle of Jack. Then, shooting me a look with his brown puppy dog eyes, "You mind?"

"It's your liver, Elvis."

I assist him with removing the coffee cup lid. Spilling some of the coffee out the window to make room, he then pours two or three shots into the cup, filling it back up. I help him once more with pressing the lid back down onto the paper cup.

"Go ahead. Drink. Those trembling hands are making me nervous."

He steals a generous drink of the whiskey-laced coffee. After only a few seconds, you can feel him deflating. As for his hands, they stop shaking. Reaching around into the back seat, I grab a manila envelope and open it. I pull out the pictures I snapped yesterday afternoon across the river in Columbia County. The rural town of Kinderhook, to be precise. The town where Mr. Hills' current illicit love is still living with her husband inside a doublewide trailer set on a two acre streamside parcel, while spending her mornings balling the mailman and her late afternoons getting it on with the present and accounted for facsimile of Elvis Presley. *Fat* Elvis.

"Read 'em and weep, Elvis. She ain't nothin but a hound dog, anyway."

He sets his spiked coffee onto the dash, snatches the

pics from my hand, slaps them face-down onto his lap. He lifts the first one, and with his right hand having resumed its trembling, turns it over. The photo reveals his girlfriend's heart-shaped naked posterior. It's pointed up in the air while she bends over in preparation for rear-entry by the mailman, whose blue uniformed pants and tighty-whitey BVDs are wrapped around his white tennis sock-covered ankles. I have to admit, it isn't a bad live shot for an amateur photographer. The focus is perfect and I even snapped the pic as the blonde bombshell is looking over her shoulder, no doubt saying something profound to the mailman. Something like, "Do me...do me...I can't wait any longer."

The rest of the photos are simply different versions of the same shot. You seen one pic of an over-sexed thirty-something blonde taking it doggy style in her backyard from the mailman, you've sort of seen them all. But that doesn't prevent Roland Hills from studying each and every single one of them like he's looking at the most recent issue of *Penthouse Magazine*. You know, holding them only inches from his face, turning them one way, then the other.

When he's done, he slaps the pics back down onto his lap. It's then I see he's crying like a baby. Tears streaming down his fat cheeks, he opens his mouth wide and begins to sing at the top of his lungs, *"We're caught in a trap...I can't walk out...Because I love you too much, baby!"*

I'll be dipped. He's starting to make a scene. But I gotta give him credit. If I close my eyes, it really does sound like I'm blaring the late king of rock 'n' roll on the hearse's old eight-track stereo system. Hills is so good, a group of blue-jeaned construction workers gather around the black hearse. They clap and cheer as soon as the crying, fake Elvis issues his last tearful note. One big guy with a brush cut even raises up his cigarette lighter, thumbing a flame.

"You're building your fan base, Elvis."

He wipes the tears from his eyes with the back of his meaty hand.

"I don't want new fans. I want my Betty back."

Betty Reddy. That's his cheating girlfriend's name and it's no joke. 'Course, if you close your eyes and say it out loud, you get the full effect.

Betty Reddy...bet all the guys called her Betty Reddy Beaver in high school. Or maybe Betty Reddy for cock...no wonder she's addicted to sex.

"She wasn't yours to begin with. Go back to your wife."

"Lorraine won't have me back. She filed for divorce three days ago."

"Beg for forgiveness. Tell her you strayed if only to realize what you had right before your eyes. Works like a charm every time."

He's quiet for a minute while sad-faced workers stroll in and out of the coffee shop. Then, "You have a girlfriend, Mr. Moonlight? Someone special in your life?"

I shake my head, sip my coffee.

"No," I say, the vision of a beautiful brunette, my now dead ex, Lola, filling my head. "Not at present."

"Funny you giving me advice. Man with a hunk of metal in his brain and no woman." Slamming his barrel chest with his fist. "You could drop dead today. But I got my whole life to live. And I wanted to live it with Betty."

My eyes lock on his.

"You have a real way with words, Elvis." Leaning down, I gather up my pics, stuff them back into the envelope. "Don't lose your day job."

He opens the door, grabs his coffee, proceeds to step on out. But I take hold of his arm. It's skinny, bony even. Totally out of synch with the rest of his body.

"I believe you owe me something, Elvis. An even grand, plus expenses. You can deduct the coffee if you want."

He turns to me, his big brown eyes blinking.

"I've sort of run into a bit of problem." His teary eyed frown turns upside down. "You see, Mr. Moonlight, since the telephone company found out about me and Betty, we both been handed our walking papers."

"You telling me you can't pay me?"

There it is again, the minus zero bank balance, the account getting colder and colder as it becomes emptier...

"Not now anyway." Then, perking up. "But hey, I've got an idea. You got any party plans in the future? Elvis and the Teddy Bears does parties, weddings, and bar mitzvahs. You'd get yourself a half price deal."

"You kidding me, Elvis?"

"Half price is at least worth one thousand."

And that's when my entire blood supply spills out onto the hearse floor. I see her. Through the windshield. Walking into the coffee shop. I see her.

I. See. Her.

A tall woman. Her brunette hair is rich and long. Her body is taller and leaner than I remember. But not skinny. She's wearing tight jeans, sandals, a long sleeved loose-fitting shirt with a deep V-neck, exposing the tan skin that covers her firm breasts. Two or three silver necklaces drape down from her neck, and further draw my attention to the exposed skin on her chest. Her lips are thick and red. They form a heart when she presses them together. Her nose is so perfect, it seems as though it were carved out of stone by a master artist. Covering her eyes, dark aviator sunglasses.

Lola.

But how can it be Lola?

Lola died.

I left Lola lifeless, laying on highway cement between New York City and Albany. She had breathed her last and the spark had exited her body. I saw it happen. I was there. I walked away from her death, and I never looked back. Not even once.

Maybe I should have.

"You okay, Mr. Moonlight?"

Elvis talking, prodding me with his index finger. Like I've suddenly gone catatonic. And I have.

"No. I'm not alright." I hold out my hand. "Whiskey."

He hands me the bottle. I uncap it, take a deep drink, hand it back without capping it.

He takes it in hand, then grabs the cap, screwing it back on. "Jeez, that was supposed to last me all day."

I want to get out of the hearse. I want to head into the store. I want to see if my eyes are deceiving me. But I can't fucking move.

"You want me to get you a drink of water, Moonlight?"

I turn to Elvis.

"Take your pictures. We're done here."

"You okay with an I.O.U.?"

"Yeah. Just go. I'll call you if I need something."

The door opens and Elvis gets out. Several of the onlookers who heard him singing issue him a second round of applause. Elvis bends at the waist, bows to his new peeps. Then, straightening himself back up, he reaches into his jean pocket and proceeds to hand out business cards.

"The King is back in town," he barks in his best trembling imitation of Elvis's voice. "Available for birthday parties, weddings, retirement parties, bar mitzvahs, and a whole lot more."

The door to the store opens again. She walks out. My heart beats in my throat, adrenalin pumping through the veins in my head. I want to get out of the car, but I'm glued to the seat. Glued because I have to either be seeing things, or my judgment is entirely off. Like I said, I've got a piece of .22 caliber bullet lodged in my brain. It causes me problems from time to time. Brain problems. I'm not just a head-case. I'm Captain Head-Case.

But there she is. Lola. In the flesh.

She briefly holds the door open for an elderly man who limps on through. Then, turning her back to me, she walks away in the opposite direction.

My Lola walks away.

Chapter 2

I take a moment to catch my breath before I hyperventilate. Long enough for the morning nine to five, working-stiff rush to dissipate, leaving the coffee shop parking lot empty.

From a distance, I watch her slip behind the wheel of a newer model, black Lexus. Watch her take a quick sip of her coffee, then set it into the center console cup holder before she starts the car, backs out. Watch her slowly make the short drive to the exit where she carefully looks both ways prior to hooking a slow left onto Broadway, in the direction of North Albany.

Maybe I should follow her. Maybe I should get my shit together and tail her for a while. But then, what if I'm wrong? What if the woman I just saw going in and out of the coffee joint only *looked* like Lola? If that does indeed turn out to be the truth, then I am destined to be even more lonely and broken hearted than I already am.

It's only been a matter of months since I left her there, dead, on the road. What if I were to chase the woman in the aviator sunglasses down and she only turns out to be a Lola lookalike? I'll lose the love of my life a second time. But that's fucking whack. Is it possible I'd rather *not* confirm the fact that Lola lives more than I would want to reconfirm her death? Where's the sense in that? But then, it's Dick Moonlight here. I haven't got the sense to come in out of the rain. That is, if it were raining in the first place.

I start the hearse, back out of the spot. Throwing the big tranny in drive, I make it across the lot to the exit.

Which leaves me with a choice. I can go left on Broadway, try and find the black Lexus, or I can turn right, head on back to my riverside loft in time for my meeting with a prospective client. A paying client.

Peeling my right hand from off the steering wheel, I place it over my heart, like I hope to die. I'll let my heart decide. I can feel it pounding, bleeding, through my leather coat, through my flesh and ribs. My heart is crying for Lola with every beat.

Chase heartache or a paycheck? Which way?

What if the woman in the Lexus is not her?

I punch the gas, go right.

Chapter 3

He's already waiting for me as I drive up to the old, two-story brick building inside the abandoned Port of Albany. He's a short, pudgy guy wearing an expensive suit that does little to hide his beer gut. But then, judging by the Cheshire Cat smile painted on his round, clean-shaven face, I'm not sure he gives a fuck. Resting idle behind him is a black BMW. A four-door model with a sunroof that's opened. He's got vanity plates. Go figure. They say BRAINRX.

"Mr. Moonlight, I presume?" He holds out his right hand. His smile is so wide and bright, it hurts me to look at it. I look at the hand instead.

"Dr. Schroder."

He's still holding out his hand. I guess that means I have to shake it. I do it. It's cold and wet and soft. Not like a dead fish. More like a live eel. I want to make it a quick shake, but he won't let go. He's still smiling, and his eyes are gleaming as they look out at me not through normal eye sockets but two narrow slits cut into the top of his nearly hairless round pumpkin head.

I yank my hand away.

"Jeez Louise," he hisses, his slit covered eyes brighter and his smile wider. He takes a step back, looks me over. Up and down, too. "Bruce Willis."

"Excuse me?"

"I've just hired Bruce Willis to be my driver. Could that be anymore apropos?"

"That's what I am? Your driver? You can call the local livery labor pool for that."

11

"Well, I might also require some occasional brawn to go with the driving part. Things have been...let's just say...difficult."

"Your arrest."

He takes a step forward, shoots me a look while cocking his head. His smile is still there only it's diminished somewhat. I've touched a nerve.

"Oh, but I'm soooo innocent. Sooooo wrongly accused."

"That so, Doctor." It's a question. Like I don't believe him for shit. And why should I? I did some background checking on the apparently wealthy brain surgeon. Seems he enjoys living on the wild side. The swinger life. No one within his immediate vicinity has been immune to it. Even his now former Polish housekeeper complained about him answering the door to his North Albany mansion in the nude.

So here's what I else I already know about the good doctor who wants me to drive him around: the cops have revoked his license due to his third DWI in as many years. He's fifty-three years old. Divorced, with an eighteen-year-old son. He likes to drink and party. Hence the DWIs. And, as I mentioned previously, he likes to toss his dick around, too. But then, that kind of thing tends to go with power, money, prestige, being born with a silver spoon in your mouth and up your ass. A graduate of a local country day-prep school, he also attended Yale, where his dad, also a brain surgeon and founder of the family practice, was the head of his class. The son, however, did not fare as well, having flunked out on two separate occasions. Somehow Yale saw fit to reinstate him and somehow each time they did, a new pavilion, or student union, or parking lot, or sports complex would be constructed. Thank God for the old boy network.

My job, as it was offered by Dr. Schroder, is to drive

him around for a few days, until his license is once more reinstated, which shouldn't be that difficult for a man of his means, not to mention lawyer and judge connections. For my services I get my daily three hundred rate, plus expenses. Not bad, especially coming off a gig where I had to spend three days and nights watching a beautiful woman getting it on with the mailman. Still, easy money or no easy money, Richard "Dick" Moonlight himself isn't that easy. Or so I like to believe. Considering this man's profession, I intend for him to sweeten the pot before I issue the definitive "yes." After all, the payday on my mailman/Elvis gig has officially been placed in the pending bin.

"The police have a problem with successful citizens, Mr. Moonlight, wouldn't you agree?"

"I wouldn't know, Doc. About the successful part, that is."

"You seem to be doing well, as a self-employed investigative professional."

"Thought you were hiring me as a driver."

"I am. But like I've already intuited, maybe also as a bit of a bodyguard. If you get my drift."

A light bulb flashes off in my fragile brain.

"You got some enemies out there, Doc? Besides the APD? That what this exercise is about?"

He tilts his head to the side again. And he's still smiling. Staring at me with black eyes through those thin horizontal cracks. It's unnerving.

"Let's just say I've made a couple of bad business decisions lately."

I just stare at him. Into him.

He laughs, pats me on the back like I'm his good buddy. "Don't worry. Nothing's going to happen. Not with you around. Mr. Bruce 'Bad Ass' Willis."

I point at my head with my index finger, like I'm imitating a man holding a gun to his head.

"And you know about my brain?"

"Oh yes, yes I do. I'm a brain surgeon. We're all aware of your, ummm, little problem. But why don't you give me your personal take on it? Should I be worried?"

"I have a piece of bullet planted in my brain directly beside my cerebral cortex. I've been told it's inoperable. I could die at any time, or fall into a coma, or simply pass out, even while driving you around. I also tend to forget things during moments of stress. That about sums it up."

More staring.

"If I take your job on, Doc, would you be willing to give my head another look? Look under the hood for me? Maybe you'll see something no else has before. A way to open me up, get at that bullet once and for all. Before it finally shifts the wrong way and kills me off."

He gives me that look again. Like he's undressing me. Moonlight the creeped out.

"I would be happy to look inside that head of yours, no charge. Do we have a deal?"

I nod. Then, "I assume we'll be using your ride?"

"Indeed. Hope you like Beemers."

"I'm used to hearses. But it will do."

He steals a glance at Dad's hearse.

"Odd ride you got there, Mr. Moonlight. But to each his own."

"It's paid for. And it constantly reminds me life on this little blue planet can be fleeting."

"How poetic, Mr. Moonlight. But you might look on the bright side of life once in a while. You look plenty healthy to me." Placing his cold right hand on my left arm. "I shall enjoy riding around with you for a few days...Bruce."

"And I shall enjoy taking your money...Doc."

Chapter 4

First I adjust the driver's seat to accommodate my longer legs. Then I shoot the doc a look.

"Where to?"

He shoots me a look back, his top teeth biting down on his thin bottom lip.

"I can think of a few places, Bruce," he says, with a wink of his eye.

Okay, I'm thick, but not that thick.

"Doc," I say, "I'm no homophobe, but I can tell you this. I don't do men."

He laughs.

"Jesus, Moonlight. Learn to live a little. I'm not a fag. I enjoy a beautiful woman like any other red blooded man." He shrugs his shoulders. "But sometime, a hole is a hole. Especially when it belongs to Bruce Willis."

God, poor Bruce. I turn the key. The engine comes to life, purrs.

"Too bad for you," he adds. "Too bad for me."

"Hope you don't mind my saying so, Doc. But you got some real issues."

I drive out of the abandoned port lot, with no specific destination in mind other than my bank account.

Chapter 5

We're not driving for another ten seconds before the doctor tells me to pull over at the same coffee shop where less than an hour ago I witnessed the would-be resurrection of my old lover, Lola Ross. But that's crazy. The woman I saw only looked like her. Because no way Lola could be alive. Rather, no way could she still be alive and not attempt to make contact with me. I was the love of her life. Head-case or no head-case, Lola loved me more than anyone else, even when she left me for the man who, back in her high school days, had become the teenaged father to her only son. Even though we split up, I knew she still loved me, no matter what.

Or maybe I was wrong.

Maybe Lola really had fallen out of love with me and, now, I just don't want to believe the truth.

I park in an empty spot outside the store. Schroder is sitting in back, thumbing in a text with both hands on his iPhone. He's got that narrow, pink-lipped, shit-eating grin going while he's working both thumbs. I throw the automatic tranny in park, run both hands over my neatly shorn scalp.

"What're you having, Doc?" I say. "Or are you going in on your own?"

He continues texting, until he tears his eyes away from the screen, looks up at me.

"Oh, yes," he says, in that high-pitched, loosebowelled, snake voice. Reaching into his trouser pocket, he comes back out with a stack of bills. He peels one off, hands it to me. It's a twenty. "A pack of Marlboro red cigarettes," he says. "And a six-pack of Heineken beer. Got that, Bruce?"

"Don't call me Bruce," I say, taking the twenty in hand. "Didn't figure you for a smoker or a day drinker."

"Oh, it's not for me. I'm on the wagon after the last DWI. It's for my son."

"Your son," I say. It's a question.

"Oh, don't worry. He's a senior." He's back to furiously texting. "I'm talking to the tiger right now. After you get the goods, we'll go pick him up from school."

I nod. Kid must be older than eighteen and he must go to the state college. Kind of a downfall from grace, you ask me. Two generations of Yale grads and the third in line is roughing it at the local college. But the old man doesn't seem too upset over the kid's apparent break with tradition, considering he's ponying up for the alcohol and tobacco. Oh, well, ours is not to wonder why.

I get out of the car, head into the store to buy cigs and beer. At ten o'clock in the morning.

When I make my return to the car, I find the doc is on the phone. His dark eyes are wide and bulging out of their slits. His smile is back and he's talking a mile a minute. The windows and sunroof are open so I'm able to catch some of what's being said.

"Have I ever let you good folks down? You know I'll deliver. You know you can trust me. Tonight, nine sharp, in the parking lot of the St. Pius church up in Loudonville. Now tell me, how are you liking America

17

these days?"

That's when I make like a frog in my throat, open the driver's side door, toss the plastic bag of beer and smokes onto the passenger side seat.

"Gotta go," the surgeon spits into the iPhone, killing the connection.

"Got a date tonight, Doc?" I say, shutting the door, restarting the engine.

"Oh, I don't date anymore. Not since I found the love of my life."

"The love of your life. Good for you, Doc."

I back out of the lot, head back toward Broadway.

"Yes, yes," he says. "The sister-in-law of a senator and very, very sexy. She has an extremely open attitude toward the sexual act. Very modern, you might say. Met her after my first DWI."

"How ironical," I say.

"You have a way with words, Bruce," he giggles. "Take a right on Broadway."

I do it.

"Albany State campus?" I pose, my eyes connecting with his in the rearview.

"No. My son is in high school. My old day-prep school, as a matter of fact. The Albany Academy."

So the Schroder boy is only eighteen after all...

I glance at the beer and the smokes. Once more I'm reminded it's only a little after ten in the morning. Moonlight the observant.

"Your boy have a doctor appointment?" I say.

"Haha," he says. "No. He's been suspended. Crazy kid."

"Suspended, and you're buying him beer?"

"Kids will be kids. Don't you think, Bruce? Best to not make a big deal out of a little thing."

"He got suspended for a little thing?"

"His girlfriend screamed date rape during a party I

18

threw for the kids at the house this past weekend and now the entire school board has their panties in one gigantic orgy of a twist. Can't tell you how many times I was suspended from the same school, and look how I turned out. In my day, no meant yes."

I make eye contact with his beady eyes once more, and it's all I can do to peel my gaze away from the mirror.

"You got a point, Doc," I say, driving in the direction of the prep school. "Look how good you turned out."

Chapter 6

I've driven past The Albany Academy for Boys maybe a million and one times since I've lived in New York's capital city, but never really taken a good look at the place until now. Located directly across the street from a more modern all girl's school of the same "Albany Academy" name, it's a five-story, century old, cupola-topped, stone and brick building that looks like it was pulled right out of the pages of *A Separate Peace* or maybe *A Catcher in the Rye*. There's an old wood and metal sign mounted to a black iron post at the school entry that reads, THE ALBANY ACADEMY, Est. 1813, which means the school is about as old as Albany itself.

I ease into the drive and follow the road until it connects with a circle that surrounds a pristine green with a tall flagpole mounted in its center. An American flag flies at half-mast on the pole. I'm trying to think of someone famous who might have died in recent days, but I can't come up with an image or a name to go with an image. Maybe an old teacher passed away, or a maintenance worker.

"Park in front of the steps," Schroder says.

I do it. I kill the engine while he opens the door, steps out.

"I'll be right back, Bruce," he says through the open door before shutting it.

Out the passenger window, I watch his bulbous body bounce up the marble staircase on his way to a big white wooden door. When he opens the door and disappears inside, I decide to make myself useful. Reaching over to his glove box, I open it. There's the standard glossy BMW driver's manual inside. Also, a leather folder containing his registration and proof of insurance. But it's the thing I find behind those two items that sparks my investigative interest. It's a black Glock 36 Slimline model. Small enough to fit inside a vest or a suit jacket pocket without being noticed, but big enough to carry six 9mm rounds. Not a bad weapon for a woman to conceal in her purse, or a brain surgeon who goes both ways to store in his glove-box, or inside the waistband of his tighty whiteys for that matter. I can only assume he wasn't carrying this lethal little gem on his person when he got busted for drinking and driving the other night.

The big school door opens up again.

I shove the pistol back inside the box, slap the lid closed, slide back over behind the wheel. I hear two sets of footsteps slapping the marble on their way back down the stairs. When I see them through the glass it's like I'm seeing double. Schroder Sr. and his much younger clone.

I can tell they're arguing about something because for the first time since I've met him, Schroder's got this sour puss going. Through the sour puss, he's babbling a mile a minute at the kid, but doing so under his breath. And the kid is smirking, rolling his own set of dark eyes around inside his own set of slits carved out of his own pumpkin head.

The kid opens up the passenger door, plops himself down inside. "You get my beer?"

"I don't believe we've met," I say.

He's got his Albany Academy blue blazer on. I know it's an official Albany Academy blazer because it's got a red and black "AA" patch sewn over the left breast pocket. It's got some condiment stains on it. Ketchup *and* mustard. Under that he's wearing a standard white

21

cotton button-down. More stains grace the front of it. He also sports a black and red-striped rep tie. The knot hangs "Fuck You" low on his baby-fat filled chest. More stains.

I can also see that for a T-shirt he's chosen the image of Al Pacino in *Scarface*. The image of the black-suited, scar-faced drug kingpin firing the crap out of a black M16 is clearly visible through the light cotton fabric of the kid's button down. The boy is clean-shaven if not baby-faced, so I'm guessing he doesn't need to shave much of anything. He's wearing Ray-Ban "I'm looking right through you" wrap-around sunglasses and the hair that's showing underneath his extra-wide-ghetto-brimmed New York Yankees baseball cap, with the gold tag stuck on the brim, is blond. It's about the only thing separating him from his father. Maybe his mother is a blonde. Poor woman.

Schroder gets into the back. "Mr. Moonlight, please meet my son, Stephen." He's back to sporting that fake, carved pumpkin smile.

"Nice to meet you, Stephen," I say, without offering my hand.

"That so," the kid says. He's already got a cigarette between his lips and a cold beer between his legs. He reaches into the pocket of his tan khakis, digs out a Bic lighter, fires up the smoke, draws a deep drag. Then he thumbs open the beer, steals a long pull on it. It's twenty after ten in the morning. A Monday. But I'm sure it's five o'clock somewhere and heading toward Tuesday.

"You gonna drive or what?" the kid says.

"Nope," I say.

He swipes his left hand at the keyed ignition, as though to start the engine. But I snatch his hand halfway there. He yanks it out of my grip.

"Fuck you, pal," he says. "You're just the hired help. Now drive."

"Stephen, that's a no-no," the doc scolds from the back. But it's like pissing into the ocean.

"While we're on the subject," I add, "nobody drinks and smokes in the car when I'm driving."

The kid looks taken aback. He drags on the cig and releases a blue cloud directly into my face.

"Where'd you get this clown, Dad?" he says. "Maybe you should fire him." Then, turning back to me, he raises up his left hand, makes like a pistol with his index and middle fingers extended and his thumb standing straight up. "You wanna fuck with me? Okay," he says in a passable Tony *Scarface* Montana, pig Latin accent. "You wanna play rough?" He points the faux pistol at my head. "Okay. Say hello to my *leetle frien*'!" He pokes my head with his pistol barrel fingers.

His face feels like mush when I back-hand it, crushing his cig and spilling his beer into his lap. The ghetto baseball cap goes crooked on his head and the right lens on his sunglasses pops out.

"Jesus fucking Christ!" he shouts. "Nobody does that to me! Daddy! Daddy!"

Schroder remains surprisingly calm, as if he's been wanting to do the same thing for a long time but hasn't been able to work up the balls.

"Now, Stephen," he scolds, "you can't be nasty to people and not expect them to react appropriately. Now let's all get along and allow Mr. Moonlight to do his job. You can drink and smoke the afternoon away by the pool when you get home. You can invite some friends over. Okay?"

The kid's got the window open and he's tossing out the crushed butt along with the now empty beer can, right onto his would-be alma mater's front circle. Stealing a glance down at his pants, I can see the crotch is soaked. I can't help but chuckle. Moonlight the merciless.

MOONLIGHT WEEPS

Turning the key in the ignition, I fire up the Beemer and drive out. On my way out, I notice the American flag mounted to the tall white pole outside The Albany Academy for Girls has also been lowered to half-mast.

I still have no idea who might have died. But the thought of a death reminds me of Lola. Lola and how her absence from my life feels like a limb freshly severed by a chainsaw...*Scarface* style.

Chapter 7

The kid goes silent for the drive through Albany, as we head north to the suburbs where the doc maintains a mansion abutting the Schuyler Meadows Country Club golf course. But then, that's not entirely accurate, because the kid isn't always silent. Now and then he whispers something under his breath. With his eyes peering out the passenger side window and both his hands mimicking matching pistolas, he mumbles niceties like, "You fuck with me...you fuck with the best...fucking asshole..." I can only wonder if the doc hears what his son is whispering or if he just chooses to ignore his spawn's weird Tony Montana identity crisis.

When I enter the long drive of the mammoth yellow clapboard colonial, the kid gathers up the smokes and what's left of the six pack. No book bag. But then, he doesn't seem like the homework type. He opens the door, lifts himself gingerly out of the seat. Holding the plastic bag of beers and butts in one hand, he points his finger pistol at me with the other. When he points the faux pistol at my head this time, through the open door, he brings the thumb down, whispers, "Bang."

"Goodbye, son," the doc says from the back, like he's addressing a Boy Scout merit badge winner. "Text me later."

The kid ignores his father. He slams the car door shut, turns and begins making his way toward the house, walking with his legs bowed, like a three-year-old carrying a load in his drawers. I hope I never have to lay eyes on this creep again.

* * *

Once more I ask the doc, "Where to now?" and he instructs me to drive him to his private downtown office. I'm not sure why, but it immediately strikes me as odd that a brain surgeon would keep a private office away from a hospital or medical center. All of the brain experts I've consulted with over the years since my botched suicide—and there have been a lot of them—met me inside their hospital offices, where they had immediate access to X-ray and MRI equipment. But then, maybe Schroder prefers to meet his clients in a less clinical, less threatening environment. Whatever the case, I reverse down the drive, proceed to head back in the direction I came.

Back toward the city.

As we make our way out of his development onto a suburban road that will lead us down to Broadway, I peer into the rearview, try and make eye contact with the pumpkin head.

"You gonna let me in on your son's situation?" I say.

His thin-lipped smile has long since dissolved, his beady eyes no longer so glossed over with optimism. Can't say I blame him.

"I'm not sure I owe you an explanation, Mr. Moonlight," he says, while peering out the window at the cookie cutter suburban houses and their perfectly manicured lawns and plastic mailboxes.

"I'm a dad, too, Doc," I say. "My boy is younger than yours. But we're still dealing with fathers and sons here. The difficulties, the rewards. Mostly the difficulties."

He hesitates for a few more beats while he weighs the benefits, or lack thereof, of confiding in me. Clearing his throat, he says, "Stephen is...let's call him...a highly strung young man."

"I've gathered that. How come you took him out of school?"

He continues to stare out the window for a few more beats.

"I already told you. He's been suspended. Again."

"That why you reward him with beer?"

Through the rearview I see his head turn fast, those black eyes staring into mine via the reflective glass.

"Allow me to illuminate you, Mr. Moonlight. My son is eighteen years old and an addict. He's done more stints in rehab for crack cocaine and X than Lindsay Lohan. He's also done his fair share of time in juvy. I don't make sure he has something like a couple of beers and a pack of cigarettes to calm him down, chances are tonight I will find him holed up in some crack house in the Arbor Hill section of Albany. Entirely imprudent logic, I realize, but it's the only way I can deal with him and his issues."

For a brief moment, I'm wondering where the smiley-faced, fuck-anything-that-walks, "Bruce Willis is my driver," preppy good old boy disappeared to. But now I can see the profound effect his *Scarface* son has on him. Kids can be great, and kids can be a burden, but problem kids can really suck.

"Where's his mother?" I ask.

"She ran out five years ago, after he hit her."

"Sorry to hear that."

"So was I."

I go right on Broadway and keep driving until he tells me to make another quick right onto State Street and pull over in front of his office. He grabs his briefcase and steps out of the car. Leaning his head back in he says, "That's it for this morning, Mr. Moonlight. I will text you when to pick me up later."

I nod. Then, "Doc, maybe you owe it to the kid to get him some help? Better help than he's had in the past?"

He shakes his head.

"My God, Moonlight, am I under investigation by you? Or did I hire you to drive?"

"The curiosity part of my head still works like a charm. Don't respond if you don't want to."

He stares at me.

"Truth is, Moonlight, at this point Stephen is beyond professional help. It's not like I'm giving up on him, but I am hoping he grows out of whatever it is he's been going through."

"Grows out of his addictions? Out of his date raping?"

"I've heard that you yourself have suffered your own share of mishaps with the more perfect sex, Moonlight, so perhaps you will not cast any stones at my troubled son."

"I won't, Doc. You can count on Bruce Willis."

"Until later," he says, closing the door behind him, the heavy burden that is his son dragging ass on the pavement behind him.

"*Vaya con dios*, motherfucker," I whisper, swerving away from the curb.

Chapter 8

It's the last thing I should be doing. Heading in the direction of Lola Ross's downtown brownstone. It's the very last thing I should be doing, knowing she's dead and that the woman I saw walking into and out of the coffee shop this morning was not her...could not be her...but someone who looked an awful lot like her. Or maybe my eyes were playing tricks on me again. Messing with me. My eyes and my less than perfect brain.

My damaged brain.

I'll say it one last time: it's the last thing I should be doing. But then, fixation is a tricky task master. And I'm a head-case who, as much as he tries, cannot put the past behind him. Moonlight the obsessed and regressed.

I drive Schroder's BMW up the Madison Avenue Hill, past the Empire State Plaza, past the white-marbled New York State Museum, past the Governor's Mansion, past Dove Street and the three-story house where Leg's Diamond took a bullet to the head from an FBI-issued .38 caliber revolver back in the early 1930s. I cross over Lark and drive on until Washington Park is on my right, and the long row of pre-twentieth century brownstones is on my left. I pull over when I come to the one that once upon a time belonged to Lola.

From across the busy, two-way avenue, I watch the entrance to the building. Watch the front door as if at any moment it will open up and Lola will emerge looking fresh and beautiful, her long brunette hair catching the spring breeze while she skips down the stone steps in her short skirt and tall black leather boots.

But no one is emerging through the thick wooden door. There's no sign of life coming from the building. The shades have been drawn on the windows. There's a pile of old newspapers that have collected at the bottom of the door. I don't see any signs of electric light coming from inside the home. There's just nothing. The place has the look and feel of a mausoleum.

I start the BMW back up.

In my mind I'm picturing the grave I have never once visited. The grave where I can only assume Lola is buried. A plot in the Albany Rural Cemetery hand-picked for her by her father a long, long time ago. Back when the Ross family maintained an air of innocence. Before the split that resulted in the father and a younger sister named Claudia turning to the dark side, and Lola choosing to remain in the light. The light that eventually failed her, killed her.

Perhaps the time has come for me to visit her grave. To put an end once and for all to this notion that the deceased love of my life could actually be alive.

Chapter 9

But wait. Now is not the time to visit the dead. Now is the time to do some detecting. Maybe Dr. Schroder hired me to be his driver and a part-time bodyguard but, at this point, I sense a simple DWI is not his only problem. Not by a long shot. He's paying me good money, so why not use it to get to the bottom of what seems to be going very wrong in his life and how it might affect me and my overall health? Not the least of which involves his son and some people whom he's agreed to meet tonight in the parking lot of a local church under the cover of darkness. If I'm going to be driving *and* protecting him, maybe it is a good idea to find out exactly what I am up against.

Inside the abandoned Port of Albany, I guide the BMW up beside Dad's black hearse, kill the engine. I get out and make my way to a front door made of solid wood, where I come face to face with a plain white business-sized envelope Scotch-taped at eye level.

I tug the envelope off the door, tear it open.

I'm surprised to find a check inside. It's made out to "Dick Moonlight" in the amount of fifty dollars. It's signed by Roland Hills, aka Elvis. He owes me a grand but, what the hell, at least he's trying. I stare down at the check, at the hastily written handwriting, at the background image which is none other than "the King" himself, circa 1966 *Blue Hawaii* era. A computer digitized portrait of Elvis wearing his multi-colored Hawaii shirt, several leis draped over his neck, a ukulele in his hands, his thick black hair slicked back and perfect.

There's something else included in the envelope.

It's a yellow flyer for The 21st Century Elvis and his band, The Teddy Bears. There's a photo of Roland Hills as Elvis, his belly hanging out over a massive silver pro-wrestler's belt, which is wrapped around a white Evel Knievel jump-suit. His hair is smoothed into a duct-tail, and his pork chop sideburns extend over his chubby face. His brown eyes are hidden behind thick metal-rimmed sunglasses, the ear pieces studded with little circular holes. In the picture, he's got the microphone pressed against his lips, while he's got one black-booted leg raised in the air like he's making a round-house kick, the cape on his jump-suit swinging with the motion.

Superimposed over the picture is a list of dates for the band's appearances. I can't help but give them a cursory glance. The one at the very top lists the Marriott Lounge and it's for tonight. The second one down says, The South Albany Knights of Columbus Hall. It's for tomorrow night. But it's the next date that makes the cockles on the back of my neck stand up at attention. It reads, *Special afternoon appearance, Monday 4PM, The Albany Academy for Boys and Girls Spring After School Mixer.* According to the information listed on the sheet, the gig is to take place inside the basement "Buttery," which I recognize as old English prep school jargon for cafeteria.

My brain starts spinning.

Elvis owes me a lot of money. At the rate of fifty bucks here, fifty there, it will take him a couple of years to pay me in full. That is, if his checks aren't made of rubber. I'm not holding my breath. Moonlight the skeptical.

But what if I employ him as a spy?

Maybe it's the old cop inside of me, but I smell a rat and the rat is itching the insides of my built-in shit

32

detector. Maybe if I ask him politely, Elvis will poke his nose around while entertaining the young silver-spoon fed students of the Academy. Maybe he can get a grip on precisely what happened between Stephen Schroder and a young woman who cried rape this past weekend at the house party thrown by his bipolar, bisexual, brain surgeon dad.

Unlocking the padlock on the heavy industrial door, I slide it open, and enter into the loft. Tossing the flyer and the check down onto the butcher's block counter in front of the floor-to-ceiling warehouse windows that overlook the Hudson River, I take my smartphone from my leather coat pocket and dial Elvis's number. The phone pressed to my ear, I listen to one ring after another until the voice mail comes on.

It's not the traditional "Hi, I'm not here, please leave a message," but instead the voice of the fake Elvis singing "Blue Suede Shoes." *"Well it's one for the money...two for the show...three to get ready now go cat go, why don't you, leave a message at the beep..."*

I'm about to leave a message when my smartphone begins to vibrate and chime. Elvis is already calling me back. I thumb Answer.

"Let me guess, Elvis. You could have picked up right away." I say, in place of a hello. "You just wanted me to hear that silly message."

"Clever, ain't it?"

"Yeah, clever."

"You get my check?"

"I haven't dropped it to the floor yet to see if it's made of *Flubber*."

"That ain't nice. Least I'm tryin."

"I'll give you that, Elvis. Fifty bucks is a long way off from the grand you owe me. But I have an idea that might help you pay me off without having to work up more cash."

33

I can almost taste the sudden optimism oozing over the phone.

"You want me to headline a party at your loft?"

Now I can feel the smile beaming on his round face.

"Not exactly," I say. "Your flyer says you're playing a gig at the Albany Academy later this afternoon. I want you to do some snooping for me."

"Snooping?"

"Yah, spying."

"Well, all right," he says. "You know Elvis spied for Nixon. Did you know that? There's a cool picture of the two of them standing in Tricky Dick's oval office, shaking hands and smiling for the camera. Not a lot of people know this, but that's the day Elvis agreed to spy on the American counter-culture for the government. Tricky had himself one hell of a black list. Anti-war protestors, hippies, black radicals, even John Lennon...they were all fair game for Elvis. And the King had the power, plus the means, to infiltrate these people, their activities."

"No doubt," I say. "How about you? You got the means and the power?"

"Yes, sir."

"Good," I say. Then I proceed to tell him about my driving gig with Dr. Schroder. About his supposed DWIs and how he's hired me not only as his temporary driver, but also as a part-time bodyguard. I tell him about Stephen, how the kid has been suspended yet again from his school and how it might involve a girl and some kind of indiscretion that occurred during a house party at the Schroder's this past weekend.

"So you want me to find the shit on this kid?" Elvis poses.

"That's one way of putting it."

"Thought you were hired just to drive and protect the doctor?"

"I was, but I'm a professional snoop. It's in my blood. Plus, how do I know that what he's got himself involved in won't get me killed?"

"You got a point, Moonlight. To be informed is to be safe. This gig don't work out, I can join the Obama NSA. I'll get back to you tonight."

"Thought you were playing the Marriott?"

"Cancelled," he sighs. "Not enough interest, they tell me. Tomorrow night is cancelled, too. Only gig I still got is the Albany Academy afternoon mixer."

"Buck up, Elvis," I say. "You just gotta believe in yourself and work your fat ass off."

"Don't push me. I'm a grease monkey that won't slide so easily."

I rack my brain for a moment.

"*Kid Galahad*," I recall.

"You're good, Moonlight. Didn't know you were an Elvis fan."

"I'm not. I'm a fan of bad movies," I say. Then I hang up.

Setting down the phone, I go to the fridge and open it up. Nothing but beer and condiments. I check my watch. It's eleven-thirty. Oh well, it's noon somewhere in the world. I snag a beer, pop the top, take a deep, cold drink. Wiping the foam from my lips with the back of my hand, I try and assemble the puzzle pieces in my mind.

I've got a manic brain surgeon who's suffered his third DWI. He's got a relationship with his juvenile delinquent kid that doesn't even qualify as destructive enablement so much as it does FUBAR...Fucked Up Beyond All Reality. He carries a Glock 36 in his glove box, maintains a private office away from the hospital, and he's apparently meeting some people tonight in the parking lot of the St. Pius church—people from another country, judging by his phone conversation. I wonder if he'll have me drive him to the rendezvous. Or maybe he will take the chance and drive himself.

Doesn't matter.

Either way, I'm planning on being there.

Chapter 10

Two beers later it's already going on half past noon. The late afternoon gig at the school won't start until four PM. But Elvis will probably get there early to set up and to start snooping. I have some important business to take care of in the meantime.

Personal business.

I'm going to make a pilgrimage to Lola's grave, for the first time ever.

Schroder's BMW is a pleasant ride, but I'm not about to take a chance on driving it during off hours, so to speak. I decide instead to drive Dad's hearse to the Albany Rural Cemetery. The old black Cadillac is a fitting choice for this trip. My nerves feel frayed at even the thought of coming face to face with Lola's tombstone. But what if there is no tomb to begin with? What if she survived the highway crash? What if she survived and, worse, never thought enough of me and what we once shared to pick up the phone, to tell me she's alive? Maybe I should skip the cemetery altogether and head on over to the Albany County Hall of Records and search for a death certificate?

It sounds too impossible to contemplate. Somehow, making a visit to the cemetery seems the simplest of solutions. Moonlight the distraught.

I roll up to the open, metal-gated entrance of the two hundred year-old cemetery and come to a complete stop. I inhale a deep breath, feel my heart pounding, not inside my chest, but in my throat. Releasing the brake, I touch the gas and drive on in. From what Lola told me years ago, I know her father purchased several family plots located along the entry road, not more than a half mile inside the cemetery's southern entrance.

I take it slow, feeling the adrenalin fill my brain, the buzz-saw-like noise that accompanies it deafening me. On my right, I pass by a three-story brick structure built in the old Dutch manner with a steep gabled roof and French windows. On my left is nothing but green lawn melting into a thick wood. The empty lawns are waiting until they too are filled with dead bodies memorialized by headstones. I'm not a stranger to this cemetery. I used to work here as a kid, doing night-time exhumations at the behest of my funeral director dad. Why did we do them at night? So that the general public didn't have to face the reality of putrid human death, dirt, rotted out caskets, and the worms that feed on the decaying mess.

Soon the flat plains of empty grass are replaced with a field of headstones that must stretch for half a mile. I'm having trouble breathing. I'm sitting on the leather seat, but I feel as though I am floating in the air, as if I'm undergoing an out of body experience. Up ahead in the distance I spot a group of maybe four headstones I've never before laid eyes upon; they have been placed here recently. I immediately recognize them from Lola's description. Four plain white stones with the last name Ross chiseled into each one, as though if the women of the family were to marry they would nonetheless die only with their God given names. Such was the insistent and unrepentant nature of the ever-controlling Ross patriarch. God rest his sorry soul.

I angle the hearse off to the left side of the road, cut the engine. Sucking in one last deep breath, I exhale. Then, opening the door, I push myself out of the car.

Planting one black, combat booted-foot before the other, I head on up the grass-covered incline to the four white marble headstones. The grass is smooth and undisturbed so I have no way of telling which plot belongs to Lola, or if she is truly buried here. No choice but to keep walking.

When I come to the stones, I find I am stricken with a kind of tunnel vision. It means I'm pushing things. Pushing my fragile brain to its max. The tunnel vision allows me only to read one stone at a time. I read the one on my right first.

It reads:

Arthur Ross
b. June 5, 1939—d. November 15, 2012

I eye the one to its direct left.
It reads:

Martha Ross
b. December 5, 1940—d. September 30, 1980

Then I eye the one to the left of that.
It reads:

Claudia Ross
b. September 10, 1969-d. November 26, 2012

Finally, one more stone. I shift my gaze until it is focused on the inscribed name and dates.
It reads:

Lola Ross
b. July 8, 1967—

The death date is not there. There's no inscription that bears the name of my true love. Nothing to indicate she died at all. My heart pounds and my head buzzes. I begin to feel dizzy. The bullet inside my brain is shifting.

It must be. It's the pressure. The kind of pressure I'm supposed to avoid. It's precisely why I have avoided this place for so long. Is it possible she could be buried somewhere else? Not a chance. This was to be the site. It said so in her will. A will I witnessed and executed at her request. Maybe she hated her father but, for some reason, she wished to be buried here beside him. Beside her mother and sister.

But, then, she isn't buried here. Not yet.

"Lola is alive," I whisper with a dry mouth. "Lola. Alive."

I turn and attempt a wobbly step back to the hearse.

That's when I pass out.

Chapter 11

I awaken to the sound of weeping.

As I attempt to refocus my eyes and clear my head, I find that a funeral procession is making its way slowly into the depths of the Albany Rural Cemetery. I give my head a shake and manage to raise myself up onto one knee as the lead car, a dark gray funeral hearse not much different from Dad's, passes me by. There's a matching gray stretch limousine with tinted windows behind it. No doubt it houses the family of the deceased. Behind that is a long train of cars. Some of them are compact, like something a high school or college student might afford. It's a nice day so the windows are open, allowing the sounds of crying and mourning to fill the cemetery.

One of the cars has been spray painted with the words, "AAG Will Never Forget You, Amanda." Below the words is a poster-sized photo of a young lady. A brunette with long, lush hair, bright eyes and a beautiful, alive smile. For a split second, I think I'm seeing the face of Lola, as she might have looked back in high school, long before I knew her. But as my grip on reality grows tighter, I begin to deduce the person now taking her final ride in the hearse is a young woman named Amanda. Maybe Lola was cut down in her prime, but it hurts my heart to think so beautiful a young woman can have her life snatched right out from under her just when it was beginning.

I raise myself up onto two feet and eye the rest of the procession. Two more cars spray painted with the same green paint, bearing the same AAG moniker.

"A.A.G.," I whisper. "Albany Academy for Girls." The school located directly across from its brother school, Albany Academy for Boys.

I recall the flags flying at half-mast when I picked up Stephen this morning. The flags made me sad then and now, as I stand on the green grass of Lola Ross's grave, they make me even sadder. What they also make me is suspicious. I feel my built-in shit detector heating up, gears grinding. As I eye the last of the procession pass me by...a procession filled almost entirely with teary-eyed and crying teenagers...I can't help but wonder how the beautiful Amanda died.

Did she die far too early due to natural causes or a fatal accident?

Or was she, in fact, murdered?

Chapter 12

It's going on mid-afternoon by the time I leave the cemetery. If I'm to go with my hunch about a murdered student at The Albany Academy for Girls, and that news of it somehow got by me, then it's probably a good idea to go straight to the source. Seated once more behind the wheel of Dad's hearse, I speed-dial Detective Nick Miller at the Albany Police department.

When the switchboard operator comes on I ask for the veteran detective by name, picturing the tall, gray-haired, well-dressed man sitting behind his desk, maybe changing out the bullets on the nine-round clip of his Smith & Wesson department-issued 9mm. But instead, all I get is an answering machine. "This is Chief Homicide Detective Nick Miller. I'm not at my desk. Please leave a detailed message along with your name and phone number at the beep and I'll get back to you A-S-A-P."

ASAP.

That's cop talk for, "When I damn well feel like it."

I leave a message telling him to call me, along with my name and number, even though he already knows the number. I was an Albany cop once upon a time. My vitals are still present and accounted for in the database. Hanging up, I then speed-dial Miller's cell phone. Same song and dance. A message tells me to leave a message. I hang up knowing that for him not to answer at least one of his phones means he is indeed tied up somewhere. Tied up being metaphorical in this instance. Moonlight the former English major.

Setting the cell down onto the empty passenger seat, I head for the cemetery gates. But I'm not within fifty feet of the old stone entrance when I see the gang of reporters gathered outside. Both print and televised news are represented while a team of APD blue and whites stand guard, making sure no one gets through the gates. Parked behind the gang of reporters are two squad cars, the engines idling, but the rooftop LED flashers shining bright even in the daylight.

I cruise up to the gate and stop. Because I'm driving a hearse, the reporters point their camera and shoot, the flashes blinding. The video cameras are filming as the entire group rushes the gate. The cops physically try and hold the gang back with their arms and batons.

What the hell is going on?

My gut tells me whoever died wasn't just a young attractive teen caught up in an unfortunate circumstance. She was likely the daughter of some very important person or persons. And now her death is becoming a media event, if not a media circus.

I get out of the car and approach the police. One of them turns to me. A beefy man of about thirty, who stands almost a head taller than me.

"You with the funeral?" he asks.

"Not at all," I say, pulling my PI license, showing it to him. "I'm here on different business."

"Moonlight," he says, while pushing a cameraman back with his baton. "You're the crazy man with the bullet in his head. Tried to bring down the department once. My fucking department."

He's smiling at me, but I can see the anger seething in his red, donut fed, Genesee Crème Ale-infused face. The bringing down of the house he's referring to is the APD Union Pension scandal I exposed some years back, a sponsored cash-for-illegal-body-parts harvesting operation. Nearly half the APD was investing their hard-earned payment deductions into a scheme cooked up by Russian mobsters, along with some police elite. That is, until I stumbled upon it and blew the whistle. My actions not only caused a few top cops to lose their jobs, it also resulted in the then Chief of Detectives crashing and burning, somewhat literally. Since then my relationship with the Albany cops has been less than cordial, and that's putting it major league lightly.

"What's happening here?" I say. "This about the girl being buried here today?"

"Wow," the cops says. "You really are a private detective. Nice ride, by the way. You live inside the cemetery, too?"

"Why the press?"

"Amanda Bates happens to be the daughter of state senator Jeffrey Bates." He shakes his head. "Don't you read the papers, Moonlight?"

I shrug one shoulder. "I'm a busy guy."

"Well, some teenage son of a brain surgeon tried to have sex with her and, when she said no, he stuffed a sock in her mouth and raped her anyway. Then he took pictures of her naked body and posted them on Facebook. She was so humiliated she hung herself in the basement of her father's house that night. She died. And now said teenage prick is gonna get busted one way or another."

I feel the earth shifting under my feet at the news. In my head I picture those flags flying at half-mast at both the boys' and girls' schools.

"I thought it was suicide?" I say.

"Maybe technically, yes. But assisted suicide, you ask me. Whatever you wanna call it, we're gonna bust his sorry fat ass soon as we get word down from the D.A."

My heart skips a beat while my built-in shit detector shifts from low into high gear.

Stephen Schroder. It has to be him.

"The young lady in question attended The Albany Academy for Girls?" I ask.

"You're on a roll, Sherlock. But I've been ordered not to talk about it until an arrest is made. So fuck off and be gone."

"I'll need you to open the gate for that, Officer."

"My pleasure, Moonglow."

"It's Moonlight."

"Enough with the banter, asshole. Thanks to you, my pension is cut in half."

I turn, slip back behind the wheel of Dad's hearse.

"Everybody back!" the cop yells. "Crazy man coming our way."

The gates open.

I tap the gas and slowly go back through the gates. Out the corner of my left eye I catch the big cop rolling an extended index finger around his right temple as if to indicate to the local media that I'm off my nut. Out my other eye, I catch a few local journalists breaking out in laughter as they get a look at me driving away in a Moonlight Funeral Home hearse.

"So long, Head-Case," the big cop shouts as the crowd breaks out in laughter.

Scarface comes immediately to mind, his machine guns ablazin. He wouldn't put up with this shit.

"You know what?" I say in my best imitation Tony Montana as I rev away from the cemetery. "Fuck you! How about that?"

long time ago.

"My son has been accused falsely and that's as far as it goes," Schroder goes on. "You are not the police. You are my employee...correction...you *were* an employee. Now you are nothing, Mr. Moonlight. Please return my car to my office within the hour, or I will send the police after you. Are we clear on this?"

I want to say, "Crystal," but he hangs up before I can remind him he owes me for one full day's pay.

Chapter 14

"I need a fucking drink," I whisper out loud while turning the volume back up on the lads from Liverpool. Feels good to say it, to hear it. "A drink and a cigarette."

Reaching over the center console, I open the glove box and take out the emergency pack of Marlboro Lights I store there, just in case of emergency jonesing. I shake one out, place it between my lips. Setting the pack back down in the cup holder, I dig around in the pocket of my leather coat and find my Bic lighter. Triggering the flint, I light up the cigarette and feel the tar and nicotine enter back into my life again like long lost lovers.

Sitting there behind the wheel listening to John Lennon sing the words to "Happiness is Warm Gun," I feel the cigarette do its work, lowering the flame on my blood from a rolling boil to a gentle simmer. My head's still spinning from having passed out, and from the adrenalin swimming through the veins, capillaries, and nerve endings. Like I said, I'm not entirely sure why I ran up one side of Schroder and down the other like I did, but I'm sure Lola had a lot to do with it. The memory of Lola and the face of a young woman I've never met, but for whom my heart cries in despair.

I also have to remember I'm a professional, and my client's private affairs and the accusations made against his son are absolutely none of my business. But now that I've made it my business, it's cost me a simple, and lucrative, private contract. Moonlight the stupid and the hot-headed.

There's another reason for my flying off the handle at Schroder.

The reason harkens back to my youth. I hated bullies then and I hate bullies now. I was never the tallest or biggest boy in the bunch so I tended to get pushed around a lot on the school bus and in the playground. It could get pretty rough and more than once I came home with a blackened eye and a bloodied lip. It wasn't until I started playing Pop Warner Football that I began to develop a much thicker skin and some muscles to fill it out.

Then one day, toward the end of my first football season, a red-faced, red-haired Irish boy by the name of Patrick cornered me up against the brick wall of the auditorium. Raising up both his hands, he began snapping quick punches at my chest. It hurt like hell. It also pissed me off. Taking him entirely by surprise, I grabbed hold of his hair then proceeded to throw him into a headlock. I tossed in a couple of upper cuts, bloodying his nose and, more importantly, sending him away in tears, screaming, "Asshole!"

But from that day forward I was never picked on again. I didn't hate bullies any less, however. In some ways, having had my revenge on one particular bully made me hate them even more. Because now I not only despised them, I found them pathetic.

There's no doubt in my mind Stephen is a bully. There's also no doubt in my mind that he's also pathetic and in need of a decent thrashing, which might have been provided by his father long ago. That is, if his father was willing to take on the awesome responsibility of actually being a father. Or maybe I'm being harsh and old fashioned in my view of child rearing. But then, who am I to talk? My ten-year-old boy lives all the way across the country with his mom. So much for me being a good dad.

Shit, maybe Doc Schroder is right. Maybe the kid has been falsely accused and I'm jumping to conclusions based on the black comedy I witnessed this morning when we picked the kid up from the prep school with a six pack of beer and a pack of smokes to greet him.

My phone rings and vibrates. With the cigarette planted between my lips, I fumble the phone from my pocket, glance at the readout. It's Fat Elvis reporting in like old faithful. I thumb Send.

"Whaddaya got for me, Elvis?"

"That kid you were talking about? The surgeon's son? He's tearing the joint up."

Over the cell phone speaker, I can hear a commotion. Not music coming from a live Elvis impersonation band, but shouting, and even an occasional scream.

"What's happening, Elvis?"

"The kid came in drunker than a skunk, started knocking people over, screaming about how his dad owns the school and he can shut it down if he wants. He knocked over the snack table. Christ, he capsized the punch bowl."

"Not the punch bowl."

"Yes, sir, the punch bowl. I had to stop my set right in the middle of 'Hound Dog.' And I love doing 'Hound Dog.' My fans love it."

"You got fans at a high school? Kids even know who the real Elvis is?"

"'Course they do. They think *I'm* the real Elvis."

"You're warped, you know that, Elvis? Where's the Schroder kid now?"

"Fighting it out with some chaperones. But the cops are on their way."

"So am I," I say, hanging up.

Chapter 15

Fuck me, but I'm getting involved in something that's not my business when instead I should be returning the Doc's car or else risk arrest by an APD who already hates my guts. But those same guts are speaking to me. They're telling me to get to the bottom of Stephen and his dad. Because if they did have anything to do with a teenage girl's humiliation and suicide, than I want nothing more than to see their suburban castle come tumbling down. It's not a question of revenge over having been bullied as a boy or defending a now deceased young woman who resembles a younger Lola. It's a question of right versus wrong.

Turning the wheel to the left, I head up the State Street hill in the direction of The Albany Academy for Boys.

By the time I reach the round-about outside the stately brick and marble academic institution, the cops have already arrived. Two blue and whites are parked on the circular spot of grass, their flashers going, radios blaring. One of the uniformed cops is standing outside the cars, as if guarding them.

"Is Elvis still in the building?" I ask, as I exit the hearse.

The tall, thin cop issues me a glare like, *Are you serious?*

"Get back in your car and drive away," he orders. "We have a situation in the school."

Just then the wooden doors fly open. I see Stephen being dragged down the marble stairs, his hands cuffed behind his back, two more uniformed cops doing the dragging. The kid is so drunk his feet don't work, and the tips of his black Converse sneakered toes are nailing every marble stair tread on the way down. He's also screaming something in his own particular version of a teenaged drunken slur. If I listen closely I can tell he's screaming about being picked on. Could it be that the bully-slash-date rapist-slash-drug and booze addict is trying to turn the tables on the APD?

I take a step forward as they near the bottom of the staircase.

"You been pickin' on me ever since my dad fucked up that lady's head...that ain't my fault. That's my dad's fault. I ain't my dad."

They get to the bottom of the stairs. The kid can hardly stand, but he's still struggling. That's when I recognize the cop holding Stephen's left arm. It's the donut-fed cop from outside the Albany Rural Cemetery gates. The one who was trying to give me a tough time about his lost retirement. The one who called me crazy. He removes his grip on Stephen's arm and elbows him in the soft underbelly.

Stephen doubles over and begins to vomit beer onto the pavement.

The school doors open again and out emerges Elvis. He's dressed in a tight white jumpsuit with black cape wrapped around his shoulders. As the sunglasses-wearing impersonator begins descending the steps, his belly bounces up and down against his thick silver pro wrestling belt.

"Moonlight!" he shouts. "Elvis is officially leaving the building and the shit storm it houses. I don't care if they pay me or the Teddy Bears. I just want out."

"I can see that," I say, as the cops begin dragging

Stephen toward the awaiting cruiser.

Now spilling out of the open school doors are a couple dozen teenagers, young and bright-eyed and full of smiles over the excitement of seeing a bully like Stephen facing arrest. Behind me a car enters the turn-around. I make an about-face and see it's an unmarked APD cruiser. The car makes an abrupt stop and the passenger side door opens. That's when Detective Miller exits the car.

Elvis comes up beside me. I can smell his cologne. Old Spice mixed with a body odor that's been fermenting for days.

"Jesus, Elvis," I say, taking a step forward. "Grab a shower already."

"Was wondering if I could use yours, Moonlight. Now that the gig is shot to hell. And I ain't got nowhere to go tonight, what with the Marriott cancellin' us out."

Miller approaches, his eyes not on me but on Stephen as the kid is shoved into the back seat of the second cruiser. The boy has been officially silenced since having taken the beefy cop's elbow to the gut. The car door shuts behind him as the uniformed cops slip into their respective cruisers.

Miller turns to me, his steely grey eyes giving Elvis a glare.

"Hell's going on here?" he says. "It's like I walked onto the set of a Farrelly Brother's movie. *Dumb, Dumber, and Dumbest.*"

"Looks like the Schroder kid has given you the excuse you need to book him," I say.

"I helped," Elvis says, smiling. He's doing that corner of the mouth, trembling-lipped thing that all Elvis impersonators must perfect if they're going to be considered any good. He's also adopted a karate man stance with both hands held out like he's about to do a Kung Fu on somebody.

"Moonlight," Miller says, under his breath. "Can I see you for a minute? Alone?"

"Sure thing, Detective."

"Wait for me in my ride while I try and explain to the kid why we're taking him in."

I turn and head for the unmarked cruiser.

"Hey, what about me?" Elvis barks.

I stop, take out my car keys from my leather coat, pull off the key to my loft, toss it to him.

"Go back to my place and catch a shower," I say. "Wait for me until I get back."

"That mean I'm still working for you?"

"Just get yourself cleaned up, Elvis."

Opening the back door on the cruiser, I slip myself inside.

Chapter 16

For a moment I just sit there eyeing the scene through the window. I see a 1990's light blue Mercedes convertible half on the curb of the turnaround and half parked in the road. I take the car to be Stephen's. An expensive ride no doubt provided by the old man for absolutely no cost. No teenager ever bought a Mercedes, even a used one, on the proceeds from a paper route. In my head I'm adding a DWI to the list of crimes Miller is nailing the kid with.

Turning my eyes away from the car, I check to see if any messages have been left for me on my cell. Turns out, there's been several back to back calls from Doc Schroder. Go figure. He's also left a voice message. I dial *86, punch in my four-digit message code and await a voice that feels like someone is scratching a blackboard with their fingernails.

"Mr. Moonlight...or tell you what. Let's dispense with the formalities at this point and allow me to call you Dick. Is that okay, if I call you Dick?"

I hate the sound of the D-word coming from his mouth, even if it is my Christian name or a derivation thereof. But it's better than him calling me Bruce Willis. Rather, it's better for Bruce Willis that he stop calling me Bruce Willis.

He goes on: "I'm of the understanding that my son has gotten himself into even more trouble at his school where he is strictly forbidden, by suspension rules, to enter. I understand this new set of circumstances makes things look worse than they really are. But you have to believe me when I tell you Stephen has been wrongly accused of rape, and even more wrongly accused of aiding that sweet young lady, Amada Bates, in her suicide. Nothing could be further from the truth. That said, Mr. Moonlight, I still need you. Not only to be my driver, but to investigate what the hell is going on in Albany and why myself and my son are being harassed by the police. Please call me back to discuss."

He ends the message.

While I watch Miller get out of the back seat of the second cruiser and slowly approach the one I'm seated in, I think about resuming my work with Schroder, and what it will entail. I know it will entail some sort of trust in the brain doctor. By trust, I will have to go with the assumption that there is at least a shred of truth in his belief he and his boy are being railroaded by Albany's finest and he had nothing to do with that poor girl's suicide.

Some private detectives can work for a client without believing in them or their innocence. My friend and former prison warden turned private detective, Jack Marconi, can do that. The late Johnny Cochran worked for OJ without believing in his innocence and he managed to get the Pro Football Hall of Famer off. Maybe it's just me, but I need to develop a trust in my clients if I'm going to represent them and their causes. I don't always work for good money, but I do always try and work on behalf of what's right. And therein lies the difference between myself and other private dicks. I'm not a saint or a Boy Scout, even, but death can come for me at any moment, and if it happens to show up one minute from now, I want to know I can face the big maker in the sky with some semblance of a clean conscience.

Miller opens the shotgun seat door, sets himself down, closes the door behind him. Up ahead, the two blue and whites take off from the turn-around, sirens blaring, on their way to the South Pearl Street Precinct.

He turns around, looks at me with his long, hard face.

"Sure you wanna still be working for the Schroder boys, Moonlight?" he says.

"You never called me back," I say.

"I was busy," he says. Then, turning to his ever-silent driver. "Miss Albany Diner."

The blue APD uniform-wearing driver turns over the engine, surges forward.

"Too early for dinner and too late for lunch," I say.

"Always a good time for coffee," Miller says. "And we need to talk for a bit. We'll bring you back to your ride when we're done."

"I got a choice in this matter?"

He shakes his head. "I'm the cops."

"No choice," I say.

We ride in silence all the way to the diner.

Chapter 17

The Miss Albany Diner is located not far from where I live in the abandoned Port of Albany. It's a crusty, old trailer-style diner that was installed down on Broadway in the middle of what used to be an energetic community of steel mills, lumberyards, fabric factories, and more. Until the business owners started subbing everything out to the Mexicans and the Chinese, leaving the downtown urban area a ghost town of crumbling brick and metal buildings.

But somehow the diner has survived by becoming a favorite early morning greasy spoon for the construction workers heading north to build the newly prefabricated neighborhoods on every available piece of bankrupt farmland the developers can buy up for a song. Miller goes ahead of me and takes a table in the back that seems to have his name on it, even though he has his pick of the empty joint.

Leaving my black leather coat on, and the shoulder-holstered Browning .38 it hides, I sit down across from him and wait for him to speak first. He takes a moment to adjust his perfectly ball-knotted tie so it hangs a tad looser around his neck. If I have to guess, I would peg Miller for a three to five mile kinda runner. An everyday runner. A runner who needs to get his fix more for what it does for his brain than it does for his body. He's neat, if not fastidious, in both appearance and manner, which of course means he's the complete opposite of me and my old black leather coat, black combat boots, and jeans.

He raises up his right hand to get the waitress' attention. Before the sixtyish woman can make her way around the counter, he barks out, "Two coffees! Nothing else!"

"What if I want bacon and eggs?" I say.

He cocks his head.

"Order bacon and eggs then."

"No thanks. Just wanted to gauge your reaction."

"You're quite the wisecracker, Moonlight," he says, offering a hint of a smile through the corner of his tight mouth. "How's that infamous head of yours?"

"Same. I could die at any moment."

"Just don't do it here, okay?"

"I'll try not to. I wouldn't want to embarrass the APD."

"You tried to bury us once. Exposed a pension scam, right? A lot of cops went down. But that was before my time with the department. Heard you wrote a book about it. *Moonlight Falls.* Clever title."

"I did the right thing. Would do it again, too. Got a problem with that?"

He shakes his head.

"I'm probably the only Albany cop who admires what you did, Moonlight. I would have done the same."

The old woman brings our coffees, sets them down in front of us.

"Nothing to eat?" she says.

"This is a coffee only meeting," I say. "Police rules."

"Cops," she says, turning, heading back to the counter.

I set my eyes back on Miller.

"So now that we're through making out with one another, what can you tell me about the Schroders, and is there any truth to the kid raping the state senator's daughter?"

He pours a good amount of sugar into his coffee,

then slowly and thoughtfully stirs it with his aluminum spoon. I pour a dash of milk into mine, stir it quickly and unthoughtfully.

"Kid was with her in his bedroom. They were all by their lonesome. There was a house party going on. Unchaperoned by your current employer, Dr. Schroder."

"How do you know he was alone with the girl?"

"Witnesses," he says, once more stirring his coffee. "Lots of them."

"All of them eighteen and under I suppose."

"And drunk and high, too. That was the same night we nailed Doc Schroder, soon after he swerved out of his driveway at two in the morning. Plus we got him for endangering the welfare of a group of minors, and for illegally serving alcoholic beverages. You ask me, you'll be driving him for a long time. That is, he doesn't do time."

He stops stirring, takes a careful sip, sets the mug back down in the same exact spot it was before he lifted it up. I take a sip of mine. It tastes like rust mixed with old milk. I set it back down knowing I won't be drinking anymore of it. In my head I'm wondering why Doc Schroder has failed to mention the charges of reckless endangerment and serving alcohol to minors. I guess he figures a third DWI is bad enough and letting me in on anything else is TMI.

"Not very reliable witnesses," I say, after a beat. "Those kids, I mean."

"Reliable enough. Besides, Stephen sunk himself by taking pictures of Amanda with his cell phone."

"You have the cell phone?"

"We do now."

"The pictures still on there?"

"Stored in the phone's gallery."

"Same pictures he posted on Facebook?"

He takes another sip of his coffee. Sets the mug back

down.

"Fuck Facebook," he says with more acid in his voice than in the coffee. "Kids got enough against them as it is these days. Now they gotta compete with the pressures of social media bullying by the likes of a spoiled rich kid whose surgeon daddy thinks he's above the law."

"These pictures in question," I say. "They are what caused Amanda to kill herself?"

He nods.

"You've seen them?" I press.

"Not on Facebook," he says. "They were quickly removed by the spam and porn filter."

"But apparently not fast enough."

He shakes his head.

"No," he says. "Not fast enough."

"They find any of the boy's DNA inside Amanda?"

"Autopsy proved a clean slate. Evidence of Latex, however."

"Condoms might lead a jury to believe sex between them was consensual. You know, *Hold on a minute, honey, while I put on a rubber.* And now you're going to try and nail young Schroder for murder? You don't have a chance in hell."

"Not murder, since a suicide is a suicide. But the DA says for sure we can get him on rape charges, condom use or no condom use, plus kidnapping charges, a number of sex related offenses..."

Instead of completing his sentence, his voice trails off.

"I sense you're not finished with your list of charges," I suggest.

"The DA tells me it's possible we can nail Stephen with a count of reckless murder."

"Reckless murder," I say like a question. "You making that up?"

"What it means is that by posting naked pictures of Amanda on Facebook, Stephen Schroder may very well have recklessly engaged in conduct that created a grave risk of death for Amanda Bates."

"You think you can make something like that stick?"

He wraps his strong, blue-veined hands around the coffee mug, kind of like he's wrapping them around Schroder's neck. Both Schroders' necks.

"I'm going to try my damndest."

I sit back, look him in the eye.

"Why do I get the feeling there's something personal going on here between you and the Schroders?"

"Never mind," he insists.

We sit in silence for a weighted moment. Until I slide out of the booth, stand.

"What was this?" I say. "Why you telling me this stuff?"

"You're working for Schroder. Thought you'd like to know. You called me first, remember?"

He's right. I did place a call to him, inquiring about Stephen. Sometimes my short term memory isn't the most reliable.

"Actually, I've been shit canned."

His cold gray eyes light up.

"But then he rehired me a little while ago, upon hearing about his son's arrest," I add.

Miller nods, runs his two right fingers over his left hand wedding finger where I'm certain a gold band once resided.

"How long you been divorced?" I ask.

"Not divorced. Widowed. Just before I joined the APD from the Troy cops."

"I'm sorry. How did she die?"

"She died on the operating table."

I feel myself shaking my head.

"I'm truly sorry to hear that, Nick. Truly."

"It was three years ago. She suffered a brain aneurysm. The emergency surgery to repair it didn't go so well."

I nod again. And then something goes click inside me. Like when a light suddenly goes on in a pitch dark room.

"Jesus," I say. "Schroder. Schroder was the surgeon. That's why you wanted to have coffee. So I'd know about Schroder and your wife."

I immediately recall the words the drunk Stephen was shouting as the cops dragged his sad ass down the marble steps of The Albany Academy for Boys. Words having to do with his being blamed for the woman his father killed. The woman who was married to one of the APD's finest.

The detective slides out of the booth, reaches into his pocket, tosses a five spot down onto the table. He picks up his now empty coffee cup, sets it on top of Abe Lincoln's face.

"There's more to it than just letting you know about how my wife died."

"What is it?"

"In the course of your investigations under the employ of Schroder, whatever they might be, I'd very much appreciate an exclusive heads up should anything arise regarding the case I'm building against the kid."

I look him in the eyes. Eyes made of steel more than flesh and blood.

"You have my word. Even if you didn't buy me bacon and eggs."

"Let's go," he says. "I'll give you a ride back to that weird ass hearse of yours."

Chapter 18

On the way out of the diner, I spot a newspaper dispenser that's thunder-bolted to the cracked concrete sidewalk. There's a special afternoon edition of *The Times Union Newspaper*. I reach into my jeans pocket for a couple of quarters, but come up short. Doesn't matter, it's the front page I'm interested in anyway.

Bending at the waist, I see the photo of a distinguished looking man standing beside a long brown casket covered in flowers. On one side of him stands a woman who has a white kerchief pressed against her lips. It's New York State Senator Bates and his grieving wife. The headline reads: SENATOR BATES STRUGGLES WITH DAUGHTER'S SUICIDE.

I stare at the black-suited, salt and pepper-haired man and I can almost feel his pain. No one should have to bury their kid. Looking closer, I try and get a quick read of the story, but Miller is waving for me to catch up. I manage to catch the story teaser. "Amanda Bates was purportedly alone with the son of a prominent local surgeon when he snapped pictures of her in the nude and posted them on Facebook. According to local authorities, the shame was too much for Amanda to bear."

I catch something else, too, in the story. Rather, not the story itself, but in the photo. A man standing behind the Senator, just to the left of him.

It's Doctor Schroder.

Chapter 19

Once more planted in the backseat of the cruiser, I mull over the photo of Schroder standing behind Senator Bates at this morning's funeral. He must have had someone else give him a lift to the Albany Rural Cemetery. Maybe his kid did the driving. But then that would have been stupid. Stephen is currently under investigation not only for rape, but for having more or less assisted Amanda in her suicide. Or what did Miller call it?

Reckless murder.

So that's where he was earlier when I called him and he had no choice but to whisper into the cell phone. He was only a few hundred yards away from me inside the Albany Rural Cemetery. How ironic. Why not have me drive him to the funeral? I was still in his employ at the time. My guess is he didn't want me to know about his decision to attend the funeral. For all I know, he hired a cab. Even so, it must have taken some steel balls for him to work up the nerve to attend that funeral.

"Detective Miller," I say.

He turns, shoots me a look over his left shoulder.

"Schroder and Senator Bates," I say. "They friends?"

He turns back to the road.

"It's certainly possible. They belong to the same clubs, same old-boy network. Kids attend the same school. Or used to anyway. Why?"

"Just curious. On the way out of the diner I noticed the paper...there's a photo of Schroder standing behind Bates just before they set Amanda's casket into the ground."

I see the detective nodding, slowly.

"You understand now the arrogance of Schroder. Far as I'm concerned, he and his son are guilty as sin."

"In Amanda's reckless murder?"

"Amanda's murder, and a whole lot more."

The death of his wife on the operating table comes to mind, but I decide not to press him.

Miller drops me off at the prep school, which is now as quiet as a church on Monday and just as deserted. I get back behind the wheel of my "weird ass" hearse and, for a brief moment, seriously consider driving past Lola's brownstone again. Then I think about paying a quick visit to the Albany County Hall of Records to see if, in fact, a death certificate has been registered in her name. But as soon as I consider it, I put the kibosh on the idea. Maybe I'm afraid of what I might *not* find in the listings of the dead. On the other hand, maybe I'm just as afraid of what I *will* find. Anyway, it's late in the day and the hall will be closed for the evening. Thank God for that.

Firing up another smoke, I drive straight back to my loft. No diversions.

Not even for the dead.

Chapter 20

I'm not inside the loft for more than a minute before I crack a beer and guzzle it, the open door of the refrigerator shining a light on my face. Elvis is sitting at the butcher block counter, nursing his own beer. He watches me drink in uncharacteristic silence. As I drain the beer, some of it running down my chin, I take notice of his having already showered and changed back into some tight black jeans and a black T-shirt that says "I'm with stupid" in white block letters. Above the word stupid is an arrow that points to himself.

"Rough day at the office, honey?" he says in his Oklahoma drawl, as I crush the now empty can in one hand, and grab another cold beer with the other.

"You could say that," I say, tossing the empty into the sink, and cracking the tab on the new beer. I place it down on the butcher block and set myself onto the empty bar stool beside the one Elvis occupies.

"I'm a great singer, but I'm also a good listener," he adds.

I tell him about my meeting with Detective Miller, about how they're going to bust the kid for rape at the very least, and how it's possible they can get him on something called reckless murder.

"What's reckless murder?" he asks, his big brown eyes popping wide, like on one of those rubber dolls you squeeze in the stomach to make its head fill with air.

Me, shrugging my shoulders. "I used to be a cop and I've never heard of it before now. But I guess it means if someone does something that directly causes another person to lose their life, even if you don't lay a hand on that person, you can be charged with reckless murder. Maybe."

"Sounds like Miller's making it up."

"Miller and the DA. And they sort of are."

"That would be because this is a personal matter for Miller? Because of his dead wife? Because of what Doc Schroder did to her when he operated?"

"Yup. This is about revenge now."

"You still gonna work for Schroder? Thought you didn't like him much."

"What can I say, Elvis? I need the damned green. And I not only don't like them, I despise them."

"But you don't like what's going on even more."

I take a swig of my fresh beer.

"Exactly."

"Right versus wrong," he says. "You always choose the side of right."

"In this case, it's two wrongs. Young Schroder was wrong for date raping that girl and then posting pictures of her on Facebook. Old man Schroder is wrong for having allowed those kids to party in his house with alcohol and to do so unsupervised, and then to have taken his car out late at night while drunk as a skunk himself."

"But..."

"But I don't think that gives Miller the right to pursue the Schroder boy for murder out of personal vengeance."

"So you *are* going back to work for Schroder?"

"Yes, I'm going to work for him in so far as I'm going to get to the bottom of what happened in his house last Friday night and get paid doing it. I have no trouble with the kid going away for rape, kidnapping, and sexual assault if that is in fact what happened. But I do have trouble with him taking the rap for a murder he didn't commit."

"Like Elvis in *Jail House Rock*. He was only defending himself when he punched that dude in the bar. Then they nail him for murder because he's a rock 'n' roller. It ain't right."

"That's only a movie, Elvis. This is real life."

"I been playing Elvis for so long, I'm not sure what's real anymore. Sometimes I feel like I'm the return of the King."

"Maybe you are," I say, getting up, reaching for my cell phone.

"So what happens next?"

"It's almost six and Schroder will be wanting to go home. First you're going to drive me to his office so I can settle things with him and my new assignment. Then we're going to pay a visit to a certain pathologist I know who can shed some light on Miller's wife and why she died on the operating table."

He gets up. I toss him the keys to the black Beemer.

"You gonna bring that beer with you?" he asks. "That's illegal and wrong."

"There are some wrongs that don't bother me. You drive, I drink."

"How's about I join you," he says, going to the fridge and grabbing not one fresh beer, but two. "*One for the money,*" he sings, "*two for the road.*"

Chapter 21

The beer pressed between my thighs, I speed dial Dr. Georgie Phillips on my cell.

He answers after three rings.

"Moon!" barks the old Viet Nam vet turned pathologist.

I'm picturing the thin, long gray-haired medical doc working on a cadaver inside the basement morgue of the Albany Medical Center. Underneath his green scrubs he'll be wearing old Levi's, a T-shirt bearing the four faces of The Beatles in their hippy stage, and a pair of well-worn Tony Lama cowboy boots. He'll also have a bomber of a brain bud spliff burning in the ashtray and some Ralph Vaughn Williams going on the stereo. Blaring music as loud as he pleases is precisely why he chooses to work nights.

"Back to the full-time grind, Georgie?" I ask.

"Didn't like semi-retirement. It's like semi-living until you semi-die."

"Got a project for you, if you got the time."

"Always got the time to add to my grandkid's college fund."

I give him the short version of who I'm working for as of right this very minute. Then I tell him about Detective Miller and Miller's wife.

"Think you can find out the particulars on this one, Georgie?"

"If she came through here on her way into the infinite unknown, then I'll find out what happened."

"How much time you need?"

"You gonna still be up in three hours?"

"It's only six. I'll just be getting started on tomorrow's hangover."

I take a sip of my beer, set it back between my thighs.

"Not like you to drink much," Georgie points out. "Everything okay?"

"Georgie," I say. "I know it sounds crazy, but I think I spotted Lola."

Dead air on the phone. Until Georgie breaks it by saying, "She's been dead for almost a year, Moon."

"She was walking into a coffee shop when I spotted her. It was *her*, Georgie. I swear it."

"Listen, Moon. Take it easy and be here at nine sharp."

"Roger that."

"Don't be drunk," he says, hanging up.

I drink some more beer. Then I tell Elvis to hang a right onto State Street and to park outside Schroder's glass and metal building.

"Wait for me here," I say, downing the rest of the beer, tossing the empty onto the floor.

"Schroder isn't going to like that," Elvis says, pointing to the can now sitting on the Beemer's formerly clean floor.

"The kid already spilled his beer on the seat earlier," I say, opening the door and heaving myself out onto the sidewalk. "Besides, there's a lot about me Schroder isn't going to like once I start poking my nose into his business."

Slamming the door closed, I approach the brain surgeon's office.

Chapter 22

I don't sit inside Dr. Schroder's private office. I choose instead to stand. Moonlight the stubborn.

The short, portly, balding Schroder sits behind a wood desk covered in so much paper it's a wonder he doesn't get lost in the stacks. His eyes are wide, practically poking through those narrow eyelid slits. The eyes are focused not on me but his mountain of paper. His clean-shaven face now blushed red, his thin lips tinged purple, like they're not getting enough oxygen.

"You look worried, Doc," I say. "Like you just found out you only got three weeks to live."

I'm trying to get a look at some of the stationery on his desk. From what I can see, this consists mostly of letters from law firms. One particular stack of papers catches my eye. My eyesight is not the best in the world, but the bold lettering on the top sheet of white, legal-sized paper is so thick and stark I can easily make out the name Schroder listed as a defendant in a civil medical suit. In fact, the more I scan his desk, the more I notice just how many lawsuits the brain surgeon is contending with at present. No wonder he doesn't maintain a private office at the hospital. The guy is damaged goods, and that's putting it mildly.

He sees me being nosy and shoots me a look that could melt the paint off the wall.

"You really know how to make a client feel all warm and fuzzy, Dick Moonlight, you know that?"

"Hey, Doc," I say, crossing my arms over my chest so I can feel the bulge my .38 makes through my leather coat, "who said you were still my client?"

He blinks, almost painfully.

"You want me to operate on that head of yours or not?" he says. "For free?"

I think about what happened to Miller's wife on the operating table, and I'm not sure I want Doc Schroder touching me with a Q-Tip much less a scalpel. I find myself wanting to tell him this, but instinct tells me to hold off. That I need to find out more info on poor Mrs. Miller before I go tossing it in his fat face.

"Let's call it a maybe," I say.

"Then, for the love of God, will you please, please, please, do as I request?"

"Money," I say. "You might think about giving me a raise. That is, if you wish to reinstate your Moonlight client status."

He blinks again. Just as painfully as before. He also sighs.

"What a horrid day," he says. "My son gets kicked out of school, then arrested for crashing an Elvis concert at said school, and now the Albany Police Department has placed him behind bars. They're going to arrest him for rape and perhaps even murder, when the truth of the matter is the deceased young woman in question strung herself up. Now I have found a private detective who can help me clear my son and he's trying to extort me for more money."

"I wouldn't call it extortion, Doc. I think I'm worth more to you now than when I was just your driver and part-time muscle." I let my arms hang down by my sides. "'Course, you don't want my services, there are other PIs around who can do an adequate job. They'll cost you, however."

He shakes his head.

"Okay, how much more, Dick?"

"Four hundred per day, plus another two hundred

each for my associates."

He stands.

"Wait just a minute," he barks. "That's outrageous. My lawyer doesn't even cost me that much."

"Who's your lawyer?"

More blinking.

"I don't actually have one, yet. But I'm working on it."

"So what will it be, Doc? Am I in or out? You client or non-client?"

"You return my car?"

"It's sitting outside right now with my two hundred per day associate behind the wheel."

"Is that so?" he says, standing, his stomach brushing up against the pile of papers. "Okay. Fine. Deal, Moonlight."

"I could ask you to sign a contract."

"Can't you simply trust me on this one?"

"That's the trouble. I'm not sure I can trust someone who buys his delinquent kid beer and cigs or who sponsors a house party stocked with booze for underage kids."

"And you didn't party as a teenager?"

"Sure I did. But the drinking age was eighteen."

"Kids are going to party no matter what the drinking age. It's a given. Let me ask you something. Would you rather see the kids doing their partying at home or somewhere where they can't be supervised?"

"From what I'm told you left them alone."

He's back to shaking his head. Vehemently.

"The police have that wrong. I *was* home. I was upstairs all night, on my side of the house, while the kids were in the basement. I ran out of red wine so I stupidly went out to the twenty-four hour liquor store over on Everett Road. The police started tailing me as soon as I left my driveway. They stopped me further up the road and slapped me with the DWI. That was around the same time that young woman started shouting rape and pointing an accusatory finger at Stephen. You ask me, it was a well-planned setup."

"Because if you heard her scream when you were still upstairs, you would have come to her aid."

"Something like that."

I peer into his eyes, try to see beyond those cracks of white flesh, as if I could somehow recognize some real truth in what he's telling me. But then, if I'm going to work for him as a detective, I'm going to have to find a way to trust him. Even if that trust doesn't amount to a hill of stale beans.

"If you're being harassed by the police, I'll find out why. Unless, that is, you can give me a reason first."

He shakes his head, assumes an odd smile, and comes around his desk.

"I can't imagine why. Jealousy maybe. I'm successful. I'm good looking. I'm rich. Most policemen aren't any of those things. Wouldn't you agree, Bruce Willis?"

"We back to that now?" I say. "Bruce Willis?"

He reaches out with his right hand, lightly pinches my forearm.

"Just trying to lighten up the hellish atmosphere," he says.

I yank my arm away like it's been bitten by a snake.

Schroder looks at his watch.

"Almost six-thirty," he says. "Moonlight, you need to take me home. I have something very important to do tonight."

I recall overhearing him earlier, talking about his meeting at the St. Pius Church.

"Will you be needing me to drive?"

"Not at all. My engagement is within walking distance from my house." He pats his belly. "Besides, I could use the exercise."

"If you'd like," I say, "I can see about posting bail for your son. But I wouldn't count on it."

"I'm not counting on it. I just want you to look into who is acting out personal vengeance on us Schroders through the APD and why. In the process, you'll clear Stephen's name in exchange for your extorted pricing. "

"There's a question of vengeance. Detective Nick Miller's wife?" I pose. "That's right. I know about her aneurysm and how she died on the table."

He shoots me a look to kill.

"It was an accident. Could have happened to anyone on the surgical team."

"Regardless, isn't it obvious he's not a big fan of yours?"

"Okay, maybe he's the one responsible for coming down on me and my son. If that's the case, maybe you can make him stop."

"Maybe," I say. "Maybe not. If I were to approach the cop, I need to do so intelligently. Which means I need to do some detecting. I'll need to speak to some of your son's friends. I'll need to speak to Amanda's family and her friends. But first, I'll need to speak to your boy. I assume he's on his way to Albany County Correctional."

He nods, sadly. "In the meantime," he says, "I'm guessing I need to find him the best lawyer money can buy."

"Spare no expense, Doc," I say. "The boy is in big trouble."

"Don't worry," he says, grabbing his suit jacket from off the rack by the door and shutting out the light. "I'm a brain surgeon. I'm practically made of money."

Chapter 23

I follow him out to the car and, after making an awkward introduction to Elvis, we drive the doc back home. But before we get there, we make a detour to my loft so Elvis can pick up the hearse and follow me to Schroder's less than humble home. While we're making the drive from the loft to the North Albany suburbs, Schroder speaks with a lawyer named Jim Royce. He lays out his son's troubles for Royce in rapid-fire sentences. When he's done, and Royce has a chance to speak, Schroder utters, "Yes, I understand," and "MmmmHmmm," and "I suppose so," and even a, "Well, I'll just have to pay it, won't I?" But in the end, as we pull into the driveway of his home, it becomes apparent Stephen has himself a new lawyer. Maybe not the best one money can buy, but a new lawyer all the same.

"Your legal counsel say anything about bail?" I ask, as we climb out of the Beemer, and as Elvis rolls into the driveway behind us.

"He doesn't think the judge will go for it. For now, better plan on speaking to Stephen inside the jail."

"I will," I say. Then, "So where's this big meeting tonight?"

I'm trying to get a rise out of him, see if he tells the truth about where he's going.

"It's a private matter that's no concern of yours," he says.

"Is it any concern of Stephen's?"

"Not at all. Now if you don't mind, I'd like to get in

a shit and shower before I have to run out again."

"Roger that, boss," I say. "If you need Elvis to drive you in the morning, he's available."

"Will he be serenading me as part of his two hundred per day and your four hundred?"

"He'll be your teddy bear," I say, tossing him the car keys.

"Great," he says, approaching the house with the keys in hand. "My son is about to enter into a fight for his life, and Elvis fucking Presley is my driver."

I get back in the hearse.

"We're working tonight," I say.

"We got a meeting with your pal, Georgie Phillips, at nine," Elvis correctly states.

"I'm moving it to nine-thirty, because first we're going to follow Doc Schroder to his little out of the way meeting at the St. Pius Church."

"You smelling a rat, Moonlight?"

"A big, fat, stinky rat, Elvis. From the looks of things, the good doc is being sued up the wazoo by multiple clients, and he's got the APD on his ass for having fouled up Mrs. Miller's brain. And life."

"The APD watch over one another like brothers in arms, I take it."

"That they do."

"You know what this means don't you?"

"No," I say. "I don't."

"We need more beer."

"Good point. Head to the grocery store for supplies."

Elvis backs out the hearse, humming the tune to "Heartbreak Hotel."

Chapter 24

Handing Elvis fifty bucks, I tell him to pick us up a case of Bud and a pack of smokes for me. I tell him to grab some chips, too. While he's gone, I sit in the hearse and try to imagine what Schroder could have done to Miller's wife that caused her to die on the operating table. I might not like the man, but I have to believe he wouldn't do anything to purposely harm one of his patients. You don't have to be a brain surgeon to know that brain surgery is a risky business. People die on operating tables. It's a fact of life and death. Dying is the risk you take every time you go under the knife. In any case, I know that in a matter of a couple of hours, Georgie will have the true scoop on what went down in Schroder's operating room three years ago.

Elvis returns.

He opens the door, sets a plastic bag in my lap. Inside it are some Lay's potato chips and a pack of Marlboro Lights. He opens the back door and slips a case of Budweiser onto the flat platform that once upon a time would support a casket. He plucks a beer free, hands it to me. Then he grabs one for himself. Together we pop the tabs and take deep drinks.

"Private detecting is fun," he says coming up for air, wiping the foam from his lips with the back of his hand. "I could get used to this life."

"What and leave Elvis behind? Your redneck public would never forgive you."

I grab the pack of smokes, rip off the thin translucent plastic, pry open the cardboard packing. Slapping the bottom of the pack, I expertly pop out a single cigarette, and place it between my lips.

"Should you be smoking, Moonlight?" Elvis poses, starting the hearse back up. "I mean, you're not exactly healthy." He taps his head.

I fire up the cig, exhale a cloud of delicious blue smoke.

"I'm the last man on earth who should be smoking. The nicotine makes the blood vessels constrict inside my brain."

He does that twitchy thing with his lips.

"Then why do it?"

"Smoking helps me cope with life and death's little ups and downs."

"And beer."

"Yeah, that, too."

He drives across the parking lot to the road.

"Which way?" he says at the stop sign.

I tell him to go right.

"Don't die on me, Moonlight," he says.

"I'll try not to. By the way, you got my change?"

He hands me a ten, wrapped around a five and some singles. It's pretty much the only money I've got until Schroder pays me. I slide the bills into the breast pocket of my work shirt. We ride in silence, drinking, smoking, and coping all the way to the church.

Chapter 25

It's been dark for nearly two hours by the time we get to the St. Pius Church parking lot. In the interest of stealth, I make Elvis park the hearse on one of the suburban roads that's positioned perpendicular to the lot. We'll just have to take a chance Schroder won't be hoofing it up that particular road.

"Cell phones on silent," I tell him as we exit the car.

"Got mine on vibrate," he says. "I store it in my pants' pocket beside my ball sack." He laughs.

"You've got real issues, Elvis. No wonder your girlfriend fucks the mailman behind your back."

We head in the direction of the darkened brick and wood church. Making sure to stay out of the light that shines down onto the macadam from the half dozen light polls located throughout the lot, we take it double-time.

"Let's go around back," I whisper, as I head toward the single-story grammar school attached to the church's backside. Positioning ourselves between a patch of trees and the school's northern most exterior brick wall, we have a clear view of the open parking lot.

"Now what?" Elvis asks.

I look at my watch. It's ten of nine.

"We wait."

"You bring any beers?" Elvis asks.

I turn, shoot him a look.

"I'm not going to answer that," I say.

"Just askin'," he says.

Another quiet minute passes. Then a car pulls in.

From the beam of yellow light shining down from one of the lot's lamps, I can see it's a Cadillac. An old model. Maybe from the late seventies or early eighties. Just like Dad's hearse. The car inches forward past the church and toward the dark area of the school. For a split second I think the driver might drive right up beside us. But when he stops and kills the headlights, I know we're safe. For now anyway.

A few seconds later, I spot a short, squat figure ambling spastically toward the Cadillac. It's Schroder.

The front doors on the Cadillac open and out steps two very big men. They're dressed in polyester tracksuits and white sneakers. Their hair is thick, black, and slicked back with Dippity-Do, sort of like Elvis's. The one who was riding shotgun is holding a pistol, which he raises up and points in the direction of Schroder.

"Can you not do that?" the doc barks at the man holding the gun. "This is supposed to be a civilized meeting. What're you going to do, shoot me?"

"How do we know you have not been followed, motherfucker?" The man with the gun is talking in a heavy accent. A European accent. He says "We" like "Vee." I know the accent. I know it well. It's Russian. Put the accent together with the cheap Euro-trash tracksuits, the stupid hair, the old Caddy, the guns, and what do you get? The Russian mob.

The Russian mob killed me once. Beat me to death.

The doc has got something in his right hand. It's a Price Chopper Supermarket shopping bag. In the dim light from the Caddy's open passenger door, I can see the bag is stuffed to almost bursting capacity.

"I see you have brought a bag of pain release," says Gun Man. "You nice boy, Schroder."

Gun Man stuffs the barrel of his automatic into the waistband of his sweatpants, grabs hold of the bag, reaches inside, takes out something tiny...a single pill or maybe a capsule? It's not easy to tell from this distance. Meanwhile, his driver looks on in stoic silence. Like the big bronze statue of Stalin in Red Square.

"This better not be the fake shit, da?" He cracks open what I now realize *is* a capsule, sticks out his tongue, and touches the tip to the powdery insides. His eyes light up. "Ahhh, OxyContin. She is pure shit, no?"

He hands Stoic Statue one end of the broken capsule.

Stoic Statue grabs it from across the hood of the Caddy, brings it to his nose, snorts it.

A second or two passes while Gun Man waits for his response. When Stoic Statue lets loose with a smile and a slow, "Daaaa...daaaaa...she is good shit," Gun Man smiles and shouts, "Hector likes it!"

He grabs the bag, tosses it into the front seat of the car.

"You have done well, Schroder," Gun Man says.

"I believe you owe me ten thousand, Vadim," the doc says.

The Gun Man/Vadim, slowly draws his automatic again, allows the big silver barrel to brush against the side of his meaty thigh. Meanwhile, Stoic Statue/Hector opens the driver's side door, packs his giant statuesque self back behind the wheel. In the light of the car, I can see him digging into the plastic bag, like he's going for candy on Halloween night. He's got two capsules open and snorted in the time it takes to say USSR.

"We never agree on ten thousand," Vadim grouses. "Five thousand. No more, da?"

Schroder takes a step toward him.

"There are two-thousand capsules there," he says, a hint of acid in his voice. "Five bucks a pill. That isn't the street crapola you're used to, my Russian friend. That is pure stuff, direct from the pharmaceutical company."

Vadim raises up the pistol, aims it at Schroder.

"Five thousand," he says. "Do we have deal, brain

surgeon?"

I can see Schroder's face go pale. Even in the dim light.

"I'd prefer not to take a bullet over a stupid bag of pain relievers. Five it is and five it will have to be. I can have another bag for you next week. You're going to need it, judging by the way your friend is eating them up."

Vadim reaches inside his tracksuit jacket and produces a roll of bills that, even from where I'm positioned, appears heavier than his pistol. He unsnaps the thick rubber band holding the wad in place, peels off a bunch of notes, which doesn't make a dent in the stack, and hands it to Schroder. The doc grabs it up like a starving dog just handed a Meaty Bone.

"Awfully money hungry for a brain surgeon, you ask me," Elvis whispers into my ear.

I shush him and re-focus.

Vadim slips into the shotgun seat while returning his hunk of cash to the breast pocket.

"You like us to give you lift home?" he asks Schroder.

Schroder shakes his head like, *No fucking way I'm getting into that car.*

"Allow me to ask you something, Doctor," says Vadim. "Why does rich brain surgeon like you need to sell stupid drug to us?"

"Business is slow lately," the doc says.

Vadim laughs.

"Not enough sick brains to go around, da?" he poses.

"Something like that," Schroder says.

Vadim slams the door shut. The Caddy's engine roars to life. Hector gives it the gas and peels out, causing Schroder to jump backward.

"Watch out!" the surgeon shouts.

But the Russians are already speeding across the parking lot in their giant Cadillac, the man behind the wheel on OxyContin and higher than a kite.

Chapter 26

We wait in the shadows until Schroder is long gone from the St. Pius Church parking lot. Only then do we start walking back toward the hearse.

"So why do you think the brain surgeon has stooped to selling Oxy to some Russian goons?" Elvis asks as we walk.

"I'm not sure it has anything to do with business being slow. I think business has come to a dead stop."

"Meaning what?"

"As in Doc Schroder's license to operate has either been revoked by the AMA, or is in the process of being revoked. I couldn't help but notice the lawsuits covering his desk when I was in his office. My guess is old Doc Schroder has got himself in some professional hot water and he's drowning."

We reach the hearse. Elvis grabs us another couple of beers before taking his place back behind the wheel. I crack my beer, take a swig, then fire up another cigarette.

"So what's the attraction to Oxy anyway?" Elvis asks.

"It's the new street drug of choice," I explain, exhaling the smoke out the half open window. "You ingest it in capsule form, it becomes a mild, time released pain reliever. But crack the capsule open and sniff the white powder, the high is said to be better than heroin, only shorter in duration. Thus that big goon behind the wheel of the Caddy snorting his Russian brains out."

"Think the cops are onto Schroder's arrangement with the Russians?"

"It's possible. That could be one more reason why they seem to be picking on him and his kid."

"Besides the fact they're douche bags."

"Besides that, yes."

Elvis sips his beer, stuffs the can back between his thighs, returns us to the main road.

"Where to now?"

"Go left and into the city," I say, tossing the remnants of my cig out the window. "Head to the Albany Medical Center where Georgie Phillips will give us the true scoop behind the downfall of the Schroder clan."

Chapter 27

At my instruction, Elvis goes past the visitor lot to the service entrance, where we're required to stop and sign in at the guard shack. After informing the uniformed guard that Doctor Phillips is expecting us, he checks his list and confirms our arrival. Handing us a clipboard, we both sign in and then drive on into the beating heart of the medical center facility.

We park outside the morgue's sliding glass door entrance, where the old Moonlight Funeral Home hearse looks right at home. Heading through the doors and up the dimly lit corridor, we're immediately hit with an acrid odor of disinfectant combined with alcohol and formaldehyde.

Elvis raises up his right hand and plugs his nose.

"Man, what is that smell?" His deep, Elvis voice is high and nasally.

"It's the smell of the dead," I answer. "I grew up with this smell, just like I grew up with dead bodies laid out in my basement. And our living room. I'm more used to this odor than I am fresh air."

"Poor kid," he says. "Your nightmares must have been something out of *Dark Shadows*. Living with all that death."

"Not really. Death was a part of life for me then. It is now, too."

I raise up my right hand, make like a pistol, point it directly at the dime-sized scar beside my right earlobe.

"I see," Elvis says. "You're alive though."

"And appreciating every moment of it. Can't you

tell?"

We walk a corridor that's silent and yet, at the same time, filled with the sounds of a living hospital. There's the clanking and hissing of steam pipe valves and the buzzing hum of electrical fixtures and the rush of air that flows through an overhead exposed metal flex duct system. But then we hook a quick left down an equally dim corridor and soon something begins to happen. The mechanical noise is replaced with music. Not loud at first. A whisper of a tune. A lush, almost romantic symphony by the great World War I era composer, Ralph Vaughan Williams, that can only come from Dr. Georgie Phillip's pathologist's office stereo system.

The music is plainly audible as Elvis and I approach the double, opaque glass and wooden doors, the words "Pathology Unit" printed on them in block letters. I push the door open and find a big room brightly illuminated by two overhead surgical lamps descending from the high ceiling. Two of the four tables are occupied with a dead body. Georgie's back is to us, as the green scrubbed Vietnam vet and former Moonlight Funeral Home employee autopsies the cadaver of an elderly black man on the table closest to us.

We walk in at the precise moment he decides to remove the man's brain, setting it on a supermarket-style weight scale that hangs from the ceiling. Sensing us, he turns, and lifts up his translucent face shield.

"It's a full Moon!" he barks with a smile. But then, with his ice blue eyes focusing on Elvis, "Can that really be the King, back from the dead?"

"The one and only," I say, glancing at the juicy gray brain swaying on the scale, as if caught in a light breeze.

"Elvis doesn't look too good," the old pathologist says. "Kinda pale, you ask me. Here, Elvis, take a load off." Georgie points to a folding chair positioned in the far corner of the lab, not far from where his stereo system is set up on the stainless steel counter. "Moon, I won't be but a moment." He records the brain's weight by speaking into a microphone attached to his lab coat lapel, then wrestles it off the scale and returns it to the gaping hole in the black man's head. That accomplished, he rips off his bloody Latex gloves, tosses them into a blue medical waste bin. Then he removes his lab coat, hanging it on a hook embedded in the white ceramic tile wall.

He approaches us, his long gray hair tied back tight in a ponytail, his smile wide under a neatly trimmed but equally gray goatee and mustache.

"Shall we retire to my office, gentlemen?"

"Please," Elvis whispers.

"Got some goodies, Georgie?" I inquire.

"Don't I always, Moon?" he says, pressing stop on the Vaughan Williams CD, reducing the morgue to a quiet resting place for the dead and soon to be autopsied.

"Party time," I say, and the three of us pass through the door into Dr. Phillip's basement hideaway.

Georgie's office is made up of four concrete block walls devoid of windows. But due to the nature of his business, it also comes equipped with one hell of a ventilation system, making it a great place to enjoy a big fat bone of the medical marijuana he is able to legally enjoy thanks to the bout of skin cancer he underwent a number of years ago.

"Primo stuff," Georgie comments while professionally rolling a thick joint, then firing it up with a long butane lighter that looks more at home on some suburban dad's Weber Grill than it does in the basement of the AMC morgue. He hands the joint to Elvis.

"It'll take away the nausea, King," he says in a forced

voice while holding the hit of smoke in his lungs for as long as he can.

Elvis takes hold of the joint between his forefinger and thumb, brings it to his thick lips, sucks in a drag. He enters into a coughing fit, spurts of blue smoke shooting through his nostrils and open mouth.

"Easy there," Georgie says, taking the joint away from him and handing it to me, "that's powerful stuff."

I take a slow drag, exhale gently through my nose. Immediately I feel a soothing warmth envelope my body.

"I'm done," I say, handing the joint back to Georgie. "I'm a one hit wonder when it comes to pot. Anymore and I'll get paranoid."

"More paranoid than you already are?" Georgie says. "What's this about Lola being alive?"

I feel my stomach sink at the mere mention of her name. Curiously, the young, attractive face of Amanda Bates also flashes through my head.

"Save that for later," I say. "I need to know what you found out about Schroder."

He takes another toke off the joint, then wets the pad of his thumb with his tongue before stamping out the fiery end. When it's doused, he slips the unsmoked portion of the marijuana cigarette into the breast pocket of his scrubs.

"Here's the deal on Schroder," he says, taking a seat not behind his desk but on top of it, his long cowboy-booted legs dangling off the metal desk's side. "Dude's in big trouble, as you've no doubt already deduced."

"Lawsuits."

"That's just the start of it," Georgie says. "That detective you're talking about? Miller? He's got every right to be pissed off over what happened to his wife. Turns out she suffered an aneurysm while attending a New Year's bash three years ago. She was rushed here, to the Albany Medical Center, where it looked like she'd surely die if she wasn't operated on immediately to repair the broken blood vessel."

"And let me guess, Schroder was on call that night," I interject.

"And he was drunk as a hound on moonshine," Elvis adds.

"Both correct," Georgie says.

"He didn't choose to opt out," I say. "He knew he was drunk and he went ahead and operated anyway."

Georgie nods. "He went in through the anterior of her skull, located the damaged blood vessel and in the process of clamping, severed it entirely. She fell into an instant coma, bled out, and then died minutes later on the table."

We fall silent for a few seconds, digesting the weight of the pathologist's news.

"Did she have a fighting chance to begin with?" I pose after a time.

Georgie nods again.

"Yes," he answers. "Had her surgeon been in possession of one hundred percent of his wits, not to mention full control of his motor skills, there's no doubt she would have made it through without brain damage."

"How can you be sure, Doc Phillips?" Elvis asks.

"Because I worked on what was left of her down in this basement not long after she turned cold. I've got the full report on the cause and manner of her death if you want to see it, Moon."

I shake my head.

"No reason to. What I'm looking for here is motivation on Miller's part. I'm also looking for a reason why Dr. Schroder has taken to peddling Oxy to some Russian mobsters. Looks like I just found both."

"You don't say," Georgie smiles. "Dangerous

business."

"Elvis and I just witnessed one of Schroder's drops. It went down at a local Catholic church right under Jesus, Joseph, and Mary's noses."

"Classy guy," Phillips says.

"When I was in the brain surgeon's office late this afternoon, I saw a whole bunch of lawsuits sitting out on his desk."

"Sure," Georgie says. "Soon as it was announced Schroder was being sued for malpractice, and might even face criminal charges in the negligent death of Mrs. Miller, the lawsuits started coming out of the woodwork."

"Was he ever charged with anything?"

"Not that I know of. By the time there was talk of legal action, it was too late to test him for substance abuse. It became a case of one person's opinion over another. But the case was overseen by the medical board at the hospital and, only a couple of months ago, Schroder's license to practice medicine in the State of New York, or anywhere else for that matter, was finally revoked."

I stand up.

"That explains that," I say.

"But does this give Miller the right to be picking on Schroder's son, even though they both suck?" Elvis asks, while getting up from his chair.

"No, it doesn't," I say, going for the office door. "Which is exactly why I'm going to do my job and get to the bottom of what happened at that house party last weekend."

"You think it's possible Schroder Junior didn't actually rape that poor girl?" Elvis poses. "That he's being set up by the police?"

"Won't know until I start lobbing some questions at the right people," I say. "Beginning with Stephen himself."

Georgie slides off his desk, follows me to the door, opens it.

"Be careful, Moon," he says, stepping into the autopsy room with us on his tail. "You of all people know the shit that can go down when Russian mobsters are involved."

As if on cue, we focus our gazes on the two dead stiffs laid out on the steel tables.

I nod.

"I'm not careful, I might be your next client," I say.

Elvis goes pale again.

"You'd better get him out of here," Georgie says, "before he loses his cookies."

"Elvis is leaving the building," Elvis mumbles, heading for the double doors.

Georgie grabs my coat sleeve.

"Lola," he says.

"Not now," I swallow. "I just can't."

"I checked the hospital records, Moon. There's not actually anything here indicating she died within the past year. Of course, that doesn't mean anything other than she didn't pass through here."

I try and swallow once more. But my mouth has gone dry.

"If it turns out she's alive," he adds, "you're going to have to face it one way or another, and do so soberly."

"I'm aware of that, Georgie. I just can't face it right now. Can't face the possibility."

"Tell you what. I'll make some inquiries downstate, see what I can find out. I'll call you."

"Thanks...I think."

I go to the doors, once again the faces of Lola Ross and Amanda Bates flashing on and off inside my brain.

Chapter 28

We get back in the hearse. Without uttering a single word, we both fold back the tabs on a cold beer. We take a moment to drink while I light up another cig.

"A lot of death in this business," Elvis says after a time.

"Thought you were having fun?" I say, taking a deep drag on the Marlboro Light.

"I am, Moonlight. Except for the dead bodies' part of the job."

He backs out of the parking space, shifts the automatic transmission into drive, starts heading toward the main road.

I snicker. "Just wait until you get to the part of the job where the bad guys try to turn you into one of those dead bodies. That's when things really get interesting. And fun."

I can see his Adam's apple rise up and down inside his thick neck.

"Listen, Elvis," I go on, "if at any time you feel the need to call it a day, just say the word. You can pay me back for my services a little bit at a time."

"No way, man. I told you I can do this and I'm damn well gonna stick it out. Now, where to?"

I glance at my watch. It's almost ten at night.

"We're going to head back to Schroder's office. Do some recon. Then, in the morning, we're going to visit Stephen at the Albany County Jail."

"But Doc Schroder isn't at his office to let us in."

"That's the point."

"But wouldn't that be like breaking and entering?"

"Did I fail to mention PIs often break the law in order to get at the truth?"

Aiming the car in the right direction, he shoots me a glance.

"Must have slipped your mind."

"But first I want you to drive past someone's house."

"Who's house?"

"An old girlfriend of mine."

"The one you call Lola?"

"Yes," I say, tossing the spent cigarette out the window, "the one I used to call Lola, my true love."

Chapter 29

We turn onto Madison Avenue and enter into the center of Albany's concrete jungle.

On our left is Washington Park. On our right, the long row of century and a half old brownstone townhouses Lola once called home. I give the order for Elvis to slow down to a near crawling speed as we approach the one that belongs, or once belonged, to her. I don't want to look over my right shoulder, but I can't resist it. My heart pounds and my stomach constricts. The adrenalin pumping through my brain sounds like an orchestra of strings, trumpets, and drums playing at full volume. I turn my head slowly and, like I'm looking through a telescope, focus in on the windows that belonged to Lola's first floor flat.

There's a light on in the living room.

The shade is drawn over the big front picture window. There's a silhouette of a woman appearing in the shade. It's a silhouette of a tall, long-haired woman. Turns out she's not alone. A man appears. He towers above her. They lock in embrace.

"Stop the car," I say, my heart now in my throat.

"I can't just stop—"

"Stop the fucking car now."

Elvis does it. Stops the hearse in the middle of the road.

I open the door, get out.

I cross the street, approach the window, all the time listening for a voice, a laugh, a cry. Something that tells me the woman behind the shaded window is Lola and

that she's alive.
    But I hear nothing.
    Then the light goes out in the flat.
    A man shouts.
    "Hey, you!"
    I run.

Chapter 30

I'm not sure if I'm running from the man who clearly took me for a peeping Tom, or running from the woman in the window. Probably both. I don't care. I just want to run.

I hear the shout again.

"Hey, you, stop!"

But I keep running. I don't want to turn around and see this man. See his face. I don't want to know if he is the new man in Lola's life. If Lola has a new life to begin with.

I keep running until I come to the street corner where Lark intersects Madison. I don't want to turn around to see if I'm being followed. But I feel like I don't have a choice.

I turn, breathing hard, my heart beating rapidly against my rib cage.

There's no one behind me.

Then comes a screeching of tires as Elvis guns the hearse. He rolls up beside me, waves for me to get in. His eyes are bugged out wide. I should get in the car and forget I ever came to this place.

I do it.

I get in. Shut the door behind me.

"Just go," I say, pushing out the words through forced breaths.

Elvis doesn't argue.

Chapter 31

My breathing is coming and going in shallow spurts. I feel my soul going in and out of my mortal flesh and bone. I've felt this way before. It means too much oxygen is flowing through the veins and capillaries in my damaged head. This normal physio-biological reaction might not be a problem for most people, but for a head-case like me, it can mean trouble. At the very least, I can pass out. Once I pass out, there's no guarantee I'll wake up. And that would leave Elvis in a very precarious situation.

So what do I do to combat the effects of Lola?

I try and control my breathing. Try and take deep slow breaths. Try and calm my heart and blood flow. It doesn't always work, but I'm hoping it works now.

We move through the center of the city. The old city on Lark Street, lined on both sides by four and five-story nineteenth century brownstones similar to the one Lola lived in. Or lives in. The new art district of Albany where every other woman walking the sidewalk has a steel hoop protruding through her nose or a stud through her lip and every other guy sports a Mohawk.

I'm staring out the window, not saying anything, trying to convince myself the woman behind the shaded window in Lola's apartment is someone else entirely. Someone who's now taken over the apartment in the wake of her death late last year. It's the only truth I can accept at this point. That is, if I want to maintain my sanity. What's left of it.

I light up a smoke, open a new beer.

"That ain't no way to handle your problems, Moonlight," Elvis says after a time.

This, coming from the same man who needed whiskey at nine in the morning in order to swallow the fact that his illicit girlfriend is fucking the mailman.

I turn to him slowly, take a long draw on my beer, draining it. I toss the can onto the mat, knowing it's entirely possible my dad is watching me from heaven, shaking his head in disgust.

"You handle your shit your way, Elvis," I say, "and I'll handle my shit mine."

"This Lola," he says, after a beat, "she must have been pretty special to make you this upset."

I smoke my cig, nod.

"She was the one woman I got right. She was my perfection. And I blew it. I fucking blew it. And then, I left her by the side of the road when she died. Or I *thought* she died, anyway."

"You've never gotten over her. Not even in death."

"No, I haven't. She's defined my life. She is inside me more than I am inside me."

"And now you think she might be alive? You didn't go to her wake, or her funeral even? How whacked out is that?"

"I couldn't face it. I couldn't face the deceased Lola."

We reach the top of the State Street hill, the mammoth marble capital building Teddy Roosevelt built on our right, the white marble County Court on our left.

"What went wrong between you two?"

I toss the cig out the window, stare down at the bottom of State Street now lit up in bright halogen street lamps, the red taillights of the east-bound cars and taxis contrasting with the white headlights of the oncoming traffic.

"We were very different. As much as we loved one another, we were polar opposites. Or, let me put it another way, Lola had her shit together. A brilliant psychologist and college professor. I was...*am*...the head-case of Albany. Need I say more?"

He drives down the hill, Schroder's office building now in sight on the periphery to our left.

"Sad thing is, you can still love someone and be wrong for them."

"You make that up?" I whisper.

"Sort of. Or let's just say it comes from a much higher authority."

"The King."

"Yes, Moonlight. The King."

Elvis finds a parking space across the street from Schroder's office. I reach into the glove box for my flashlight. Flick it on and off to check the batteries. The batteries are good. Then I reach back inside for a screwdriver. I shove the tools into separate pockets on my black leather coat.

"Let's go to work," I say.

Elvis kills the engine, removes the keys from the ignition, opens the door.

"Never broke into an office building before," he says.

"You never forget your first crime," I say.

Chapter 32

Schroder's office is located on the first floor of a ten story 1950's era building constructed out of marble floors and walls, with a steel and glass exterior. The ceiling is plaster and the central corridor reaches a height of maybe fourteen or fifteen feet. While the overhead lighting has been turned off for the night, the wall-mounted night lighting illuminates the corridor in a dim yellow haze.

"What about security cameras?" Elvis whispers.

"You happen to see any?"

"That doesn't mean they're not there."

"Don't worry so much. I know the cops in this town."

"The cops hate you."

"They hate everybody."

Schroder's door is only a few feet down from the elevators. We go to it, me leading the way, a nervous Elvis on my heels. When we arrive at the door, I take out the screwdriver in anticipation of having to jimmy our way in. But something's wrong. The door is slightly open. It's already been jimmied. And there's noise coming from inside the office. The sounds of rustling. One or two people rummaging around the place, looking for something. Voices, too. Male voices. Russian voices.

"They're here," I say, backing away from the door slowly, pressing my back against the cold hard wall. I pull out my .38, flick off the safety.

"Who's here?" Elvis asks.

"The Russians."

"Why?"

"They're looking for something."

"Like what?"

"I don't know. Maybe more drugs."

"Maybe money."

"Maybe that, too."

"So what do we do?"

"We leave."

"Good idea."

It would be a very good idea, if the series of rapid gunshots don't make splinters out of the wood door.

Chapter 33

It's like a kid's playground game of *Who blinks first!*

Me standing by the now destroyed door, the business end of my .38 aimed up at the face of Hector the Russian giant, while the barrel on the heavy artillery he grips in his right hand stares me down.

"I know what you are thinking," Hector says, his voice mechanical, baritone low, clearly trying his best to imitate Clint "Dirty Harry" Eastwood. "Did I fire five shots or six? Well, I've kind of lost the track myself."

On the ground shoved up against my left leg is Elvis. He's curled up in fetal position, the thumb on his right hand thrust into his mouth. It also sounds like he might be crying. Standing four-square behind Hector, his partner in Russian-American crime, Vadim. He's got a smile plastered on his face, like blasting a wood door away with a hand cannon is the most fun that can be had on God's earth—besides eating Oxy.

"Dirty Harry," I say. "Excellent, Hector. Or should I call you Dirty Hector? And you don't say *the track*. It's just *track*. No definite article because track should be indefinite. Get it? If you're gonna act like an asshole, you might as well get it right, Hector."

He actually grows a smile at my suggestion, like I've made his night.

"But being that this is a .44 Magnum," he goes on, "the most powerful hand job in the world and can blow your head clean off, you've got to ask yourself one question. Do I feel lucky?"

Vadim pokes Hector in the ribs.

"It's handgun, stupid motherfucker," he says. "Not hand job. Hand job is *sometink* else." He makes a jerking off gesture with his free hand, which Hector shrugs off.

"Don't interrupt me when I'm doing the great Clint Eastwood. Do not speak word, stupid fuck."

Vadim shoots me a wink of his left eye and twirls a circle around his left temple with an extended index finger like, *Hector is a little crazy, in case you hadn't noticed.*

Yah, I've noticed.

The .38 is getting heavy in my hand.

"Now, where was I?" Hector poses.

"Do I feel lucky?" a trembling Elvis spits from down near my left foot.

"Da, da. Do you feel lucky? Well, do you, punk?" He cocks back the hammer on the .44. The mechanical noise of the pistol reverberates throughout my body.

I'm staring up at him, into his square-jawed face and his wide, unblinking brown eyes. He seems confused, as opposed to concerned, that I have almost as much gun on him as he does me.

"Now, little man," he says, issuing me a you-know-what-to-say-next wave of his free hand. "You are supposed to lower your gun and say your line."

"Fat chance, Hector."

"Listen, Mister..." Vadim interjecting.

"Moonlight," I say. "Dick Moonlight."

"Listen, Mr. Moonlight," Vadim says. "Just do it. Lower your gun and say the line and lets all walk the fuck out of here like friends, da? Like Apollo-Soyuz, 1975. Like Gorby and Ronnie."

Coming from outside the building now, sirens. Police sirens. I'm guessing we've sprung a silent alarm.

I lower the pistol, and knowing *Dirty Harry* forward and backward, I consider reciting the line Hector so desperately needs me to recite.

"Say it," Elvis cries out. "Just fucking do it, Moonlight."

Outside the doors, two APD blue and whites arrive, flashers spraying bright red, white, and blue light throughout the dimly lit corridor.

I cough a frog out of my throat.

"*I got's to know,*" I say, reciting the line of the frightened black man Dirty Harry has his Magnum aimed at. Say it while staring into Hector's enormous pistol barrel.

Hector's Arnold Schwarzenegger cyborg face lights up. It's then I know what's coming. The hammer on the .44 Magnum revolver snaps down onto an empty chamber.

I don't actually soil myself, but my sphincter muscle jumps an inch or two.

The police bust through the office building doors.

"Down on the fucking floor!" They scream.

Vadim and Hector bolt back through Schroder's office. They're going for a back door or maybe a window.

I'd follow them, if only I don't faint.

Chapter 34

When I wake up, I'm lying flat on my stomach on a bench bolted to a cracked concrete floor. Like it always does when I come to after passing out, disorientation kicks in.

"Am I dead again?" I ask through a throat that feels like somebody poured fresh gravel into it.

"Again?" someone answers. "Who gets dead again?"

It's Elvis. I recognize the redneck accent.

"I do," I grunt.

"Strange life and death you lead, Moonlight," he says. "You passed out. Must have been the hundred beers you drank yesterday."

From the way my head is pounding, he's not far off the mark. I sit up, wait for a moment while my swelled, aching brain settles itself in my skull and my eyesight regains its clarity. I turn to him. He's sitting on the floor, stuffed in a corner between the concrete wall and the iron bars. His knees are tucked into his gut and his arms wrapped around his shins. If I were Ernest Hemingway, I would describe his face as "defeated."

"What the hell happened?" I say.

"Schroder's office. Break in. Russians already on site. Guns blasting...shit like that is only supposed to happen in the movies."

"Oh, yeah," I say, recalling the office door being shot to hell and my Mexican standoff with a gargantuan, weight lifting, Hollywood wannabe Russian named Hector. "It's all coming back to me now. Like a vivid nightmare."

Just then a metal door opens and a blue uniform emerges.

"Moonlight and Hills," he shouts, as if we aren't the only assholes locked in the tank. "Or should I refer to the fat one as The King?"

I stand.

Elvis "The King" Presley stands.

The blue uniform nods to a second blue uniform who's manning some controls behind a Plexiglas covered booth. A loud electronic buzz sounds and the metal barred door clicks open. We step out.

"Follow me," the uniform says. "I'm not sure why, but Detective Miller would like to see you in his office."

When we walk through the door to Miller's first floor interior office, he's seated at his cluttered desk. He's on the phone. He looks up at us, sticks two fingers into his shirt collar like it's possible to loosen it with the blue tie knotted tighter than an iron curtain, and tells whoever is on the other end of the line he'll have to call him back.

He hangs up, stands.

"Gentlemen," he says, gesturing with his right hand for us to take a seat on the fake leather couch pushed up against the wall to our left. "Take a seat."

A relieved Elvis immediately plops himself down.

"I'll stand, thanks," I say. Moonlight the defiant.

I shoot a hard glance at Elvis. He rolls his eyes and reluctantly stands. Solidarity is important in these matters.

"Schroder's not pressing charges," Miller says, reseating himself in his swivel chair, running an open hand through his gray hair.

"What about the Russians who shot his place up?" I say.

"They got away."

I roll my eyes like Elvis, without consciously telling myself to roll my eyes.

"They got away? That's some killer police work, Barney Miller."

Raising up his hand, Miller makes like a pistol. Points it at me, like so many others before him. "You are treading on thin ice, Moonlight. I were you I'd can it before I toss yours and fat Elvis's ass back in the cage for a B and E."

"How come you're not doing that now?"

"Schroder's office building was still technically open for public traffic."

"But the lights were off," Elvis points out.

"Take five, Elvis," I say over my left shoulder.

"Good point," Miller says. "Cleaning crew had turned them out. They might have thought about locking the door behind them as well, if they weren't a bunch of uneducated morons."

"So what do you want from us?" I say.

"The Russians," he says. "You aware of any business dealings between them and the brain surgeon?"

Elvis shoots me a look. I don't have to see him in order to feel his brown eyes burning two separate holes into my sensitive head.

"None," I lie.

Miller's looking into my eyes. He's a trained cop. He knows how to spot a liar from up to, and including, one hundred paces. He's spotting one now. But there's nothing he can do about it.

"Look, Miller," I say. "I don't like Schroder any more than you do. But client confidentiality is a Moonlight golden rule." I hold up my right hand, two fingers raised vertically like a Boy Scout.

"I find out you're impeding a police investigation, you'll get more than just a night in the tank. A lot more." Then, biting down on his lip. "I thought we had a private agreement, you and me."

"Oh, yeah, we had coffee together yesterday," I say. "Big whoop. Can we go now, please? I need a beer real bad. And a smoke."

Miller rolls his wrist over, gives his watch a glance.

"It's seven in the morning, Moonlight. We got a bit of a problem here?"

"Don't know about you," I smile. "But it's tomorrow afternoon in India and that's good enough for me."

"You can go," he says with a dismissive wave of his hand. "Your ride is in the back lot, keys inside it. Close the door on your way out."

"Gladly," I say, turning, opening the door.

"Oh, and, Moonlight," Miller calls out.

I turn, my body half inside the door, half out.

"Yeah?"

"Remember," he says. "The booze. It can be a real slippery slope. And you've got that head of yours to consider." He taps his right temple with his index finger.

"Message received loud and crystal."

"You might be a wise ass," Miller says, "but I like you. You've got a pair of steel ones. Wish I had more cops like you. Be a shame to see you drink yourself all to hell."

"I've been to hell and back plenty of times before, Barn...I mean, Nick."

He nods.

"Just remember the slippery slope," he says. Then, smiling, "You have a nice day now."

I exit the building with Elvis on my tail, the words "slippery slope" repeating themselves in my head like the tick-tock on a time bomb.

Chapter 35

Walking around the back of the old precinct, I breathe in the smog-filled city air. It seems somehow cleaner than the air trapped inside the APD. Elvis is two steps behind me.

"Why didn't you tell Miller about Schroder's drug deal with the Ruskies?"

"Jesus, Elvis, I gotta spell everything out for you?" I say, with my back to him. "Schroder's my client, number one, and number two, Miller's got himself a nice little illegal agenda, which is the destruction of Dr. Schroder. I'm trying to sort this out without the main players getting arrested just yet."

I can hear the overweight Elvis tribute entertainer trying to keep up with my rapid pace so that he's forced to jog every few steps.

"So what are we gonna do now? My stomach's growling."

Up ahead, parked in the back of the lot, is Dad's hearse.

"Okay, we'll grab some breakfast, and then we make the trip to Albany County Jail to have a face to face with Junior."

Ten minutes later we're dining on plates of eggs, sausage, pancakes, and double orders of toast. Or should I say, Elvis is eating all that food, while I nibble on a toasted hard roll and downing cup after cup of black coffee, wishing I had a cold beer to sip on. While he chows down, I place a call to Schroder.

When he answers, I don't say hello. I opt instead to put him on the defensive right away.

"You might have bailed us out of jail before we had to spend the night."

"Might I ask *why* you were at my office last evening in the first place?"

"Making a check on the joint," I lie. "To make sure it was secure. Obviously it wasn't."

Schroder laughs.

"I should just fire you right now, Moonlight," he says. "Rather, fire you again." He says again like *Agayyyynnnneeee.*

"You do that and I'll have no choice but to go to your buddy Detective Nick Miller with news of your Oxy scheme with the local Russian mob."

Elvis looks up at me, both his cheeks stuffed to maximum capacity with a future heart attack.

Schroder's silence is so heavy, I feel like the phone is about to drop out of my hand.

"You're spying on me," he says through obviously clenched teeth.

"Hey, Doc, just doing my job."

"And what job is that, Moonlight?"

"Looking after you and your well-being."

"Like I said, maybe my well-being could very well depend upon my letting you go for good."

"Look, Doc, one way or the other I'm getting to the bottom of how and why that poor girl killed herself and if your son had anything to do with it. Like you, I think the whole situation stinks. But then, I think you stink, and I think the APD stinks, too."

More silence.

"Okay, I won't fire you no matter what you think of me personally. But let me tell you this: you'd better find out something good about my son. Do you hear me?

Things are getting a bit desperate on my end."

"Sell your mansion," I suggest.

"Not on your life. How would that make me look at the country club?"

"What are the probabilities of your license to practice medicine ever being reinstated in Albany?"

He exhales.

"Sadly, zero to nil."

"Take it from me, Doc, sell the crib and use the cash to move out of town and start over somewhere else. Costa Rica is nice this time of year."

"Relocation is very well and good, but first there's the matter of getting my son off the hook."

"If he deserves to be off the hook, I'll make it happen."

"Thank you, Moonlight. That's reassuring, despite your transgressions."

"Will you need me to drive you around this morning?"

"I can work from home. I imagine you have some detecting to do."

"True dat," I say, hanging up.

Across the table from me, Elvis swallows what's in his mouth. A gulp of food that might feed a small village in East Africa. "We still got a job, boss?"

I sip my coffee, toss my final ten spot onto the table, set the coffee mug back over it. Then I slide out of the booth, and stand.

"Let's go," I say.

"I'm not done."

"Bring it with you," I say, and head out of the diner.

Chapter 36

Elvis is just finishing up his hastily made sandwich of eggs and sausage stuffed between two large pancakes when we pull into the visitor parking lot of the Albany County Correctional Facility near the airport.

"You better not be getting any of that on the seats," I say, killing the engine.

"You should eat more, Moonlight," he mumbles while swallowing the last gulp. "It'd make you a happier, more likable human being."

"The way you eat? That means you should be shitting happy bricks twenty-four-seven."

"Never trust a man who don't like his food. That's what my mama used to say."

"You got a mother, Elvis?"

"Hey!" he barks. "Don't make fun of my mama."

I get out of the hearse, shut the door. We make our way through the unguarded opening in the razor-wire-topped chain link fence, moving toward the glass and brick-walled visitor center. At the metal and chicken-wired reinforced glass door, one is required to press a doorbell-like device before the uniformed guard on the inside will let you in.

"Yes?" comes the tinny human voice over the hidden PA. "Can I help you?"

"I'm here to visit one of your bad guys," I say. Moonlight the jokester.

"Excuse me?"

"I'm here to see Stephen Schroder," I add. "He was brought in yesterday late afternoon."

"You have an appointment?"

"Do I really need one? It's not like the kid's busy."

A brief pause follows. Until the voice exhales, says, "Okay, come on in."

A buzzer sounds prior to the door unlatching. I open it and step inside, Elvis right behind me.

I approach the uniformed guard, fill out the necessary sign-in sheet, and so does Elvis. After we're handed one guest badge apiece we're asked to wait inside the wide open visitor's waiting room until another guard comes to retrieve us. It takes only five minutes for our guard to arrive. He's a gangly thin black man who's dressed in a gray uniform, a black utility belt buckled tight around his waist, upon which is clipped a canister of mace and a billy club.

"Follow me, please," he says matter-of-factly as we follow him out of the waiting room, through a metal door and into a brightly lit corridor with steel doors embedded into the white concrete walls on either side. As I pass by each of the doors, I try and grab a fleeting glimpse through the narrow, safety glass windows installed into the metal panels. Behind each of them is either a distraught looking face or a portion of body covered in the blaze orange county jail jumper.

We move on amidst a soundtrack of prisoner's shouts and cries, a few of whom are awaiting their journey to a state or federal prison where they will more than likely spend the rest of their lives. Some of the inmates of County won't make it to prison, but will instead serve their terms in here. Others are here for only a brief time until they are bailed out, or a judge overturns their arrest.

We come to the end of the corridor, hook a quick left and then another quick right into an empty room that contains only a table and four metal chairs.

"Wait here," the guard says, as he exits the room,

closing the door behind him.

When he returns less than a minute later, he's got Stephen with him. The kid is shackled and handcuffed like he poses a danger to life and limb, and maybe he does. His face is pale, his eyes sunken and bloodshot, as though he hasn't slept a wink since he was transported here only yesterday.

The guard sits Stephen in one of the metal chairs, then locks his shackles to a round bolt embedded into the concrete floor.

"Stay there," the guard says to the kid, turning his back on him.

"Ha fucking ha," Stephen whispers under his breath. Then, in his mock Tony Montana, "I like your back, cock-a-roach. Much easier to watch than your front."

"That *Scarface* shit ain't gonna get you very far in life, Silver Spoon," the guard says. Then to me, "I'll be right outside the door should you require my assistance."

"Thanks," I say. "But I'm sure it won't be necessary."

The guard leaves, closing the door gently.

We sit in heavy silence for a few moments, with only the muffled sounds of the jail coming and going around us. I'm staring into Stephen's face as opposed to looking at it. As for Elvis, his eyes go from me to Stephen to me and back again. Like he's watching a long volley at a pro tennis match.

After a while, the kid's scowl slowly grows into a sly smile. One of those smiles you just want to slap off his doughy white face.

"Brings you here, Detective Moonbitch?" he says, tired glassy eyes now wide and beaming like his smile. "Thought my old man fired your suicidal ass."

"I'm still here," I say.

"Really," he says. "And here I thought it was some asshole who looks just like you."

Out the corner of my eye, I see Elvis is nervously following the conversational shootout, exchange for exchange.

"You like trying to intimidate people, don't you, Stephen? That's why you're always hiding behind the *Scarface* imitations. Makes you feel bad ass. Like you can take on the entire town with your bare hands and superior wits."

He squints his eyes. Purses his nasty smiling lips.

"This town is like a giant pussy waiting to get fucked. You scared, Moonbitch?"

I exhale and slowly rise up from the chair, rap my knuckle on the narrow glass panel. It gets the guard's attention. He opens the door, gives me a look like, *"What is it?"*

"You can go ahead and unlock young, Mr. Schroder."

"Sure that's a good idea?" the guard asks.

"Yeah, you sure that's a good idea, Moonlight?" Elvis chimes in.

I turn to him.

"Mr. Hills, please accompany the guard outside when he's done unlocking our young friend."

"If you say so," he says, wide eyes unblinking, no doubt happy to be leaving the room.

Without argument, the guard unshackles Schroder, carrying the heavy chains back out into the corridor with him so they can't be used as a weapon. Elvis follows close behind. The door closes.

"Stand up," I say to Schroder.

He looks up at me with a scowl.

"What's this?" he giggles. "Don't tell me you're trying to be a tough guy, Moonfag."

He stands, a smirk plastered on his face, his eyes unblinking, staring into me. If I didn't know any better I would swear I was back on the grammar school playground.

"Take a swing," I tell him.

"Really, Moonfuck, I eat little boys like you for lunch. I'm bigger than you, younger, faster..."

He makes the mistake of punching like an amateur, cocking his right arm back before thrusting it forward. He hasn't even formed a tight fist before I've landed an uppercut into his soft baby fat underbelly. The left hook to his nose causes it to explode in a spray of red arterial blood. He drops to his knees, tears streaming down his face, mixing with the blood.

"My dad is so gonna fucking kill you for this."

The door opens fast. The guard takes a look at the now ailing Schroder. Then he shoots me a look and, for the first time since I arrived at the prison, smiles.

"Everything okay in here?" he asks, giving me a friendly wink of his right eye.

"Perfect," I answer. "The young man and I were just getting around to talking. We won't be but a minute more."

"No problem. Take all the time you need. The prisoner has all day. Maybe even all his life."

The door closes again. The bolt engages.

I reach out, grab hold of Schroder's thick blond hair, pick him up by it, toss him back into the chair. His face is a mess of blood, snot, and tears.

"How'd a rich kid like you get to be a bully? Your parents fight a lot when you were a boy? They ignore you? Refuse to buy you a Nintendo 64?"

"Shut up," he says. His words are trembling because he's weeping. I don't recall Tony Montana crying like a baby.

"Tell me what happened last Friday night at your

North Albany home. I want to know how you lured that girl into your bedroom and what happened between you two that resulted in her crying rape, you posting pictures on Facebook, and her killing herself."

He weeps for a while longer, until I reach into my jeans pocket, find my hanky, toss it over to him.

"Clean up. Do it now."

He does it.

He inhales a deep calming breath, lets it out.

"I didn't fucking rape her, okay? I know you think I'm evil, but I did not rape her. Fuck, I wouldn't know how to rape her."

It hits me then.

"You've never had sex."

He looks down at the floor, wipes his eyes with the now soiled hanky.

"No, I haven't. Not with a girl." Then, looking back up at me. "You understand me?"

And there it was. The reason for Stephen's bullying. Or more accurately, perhaps one of the main reasons.

"I get it," I say, shaking my head. "But what I don't get is why you would have lured a young lady into your room during a house party if your preferred gender has nothing whatsoever to do with hers."

He wipes his nose with the hanky again. It isn't bleeding anymore.

"That's just it," he says. "She lured me."

"She lured you."

He nods, his face having gone from wise-ass-smug-punk to sad, deflated, and frightened.

"It's the truth, Mr. Moonlight."

"What about the pictures? The ones that went up on Facebook."

"I took them. I wanted her out of my bedroom. She wouldn't leave. She got naked, kept throwing herself at me. I told her to stop. She wouldn't. I told her if she

122

didn't, I'd take some pics and post them on Facebook. She started calling me gay and a queer and a fatso fag, and whatever. So I took the pictures and posted them. It was a big mistake because she went ballistic, started swinging at me, yelling 'Rape, Rape, Rape!' It broke the party up. So did my dad coming home with the cops right behind him."

"I can only imagine."

"I wanna be done with this."

"You shouldn't have taken those pictures. Shouldn't have posted them on Facebook."

"I know," he says, weeping some more. Softy, mournfully, regretfully. "I liked Amanda. I wanted to be friends with her. She wanted to hang out with me. But I..." His words trail off because we both know what he's about to say. That he couldn't live a lie with Amanda, who was supposed to be his friend, any more than he can live a lie with anyone else.

I stand.

"Your father know about you? Your sexual orientation?"

He wipes his eyes with the backs of his hands, pulls himself together.

"How can he not?"

"He doesn't like it, does he?"

He looks me in the eye.

"He and his old school pals used to take a special pleasure in beating fags up in the locker room after gym. Which is kind of weird since I'm pretty convinced that my dad goes both ways. Must be he hates himself as much as I hate myself sometimes. Does that answer your question?"

I see the pain in his face. The anguish.

"What you're telling me is the truth? About Amanda?"

"Yes."

"Then I'll do what I can to get you out of here."

"Thank you." He stands. "Listen, Mr. Moonlight. I'm sorry about...before. Me calling you names. When I get scared, I get like that."

I nod.

"Don't worry about it. Worry more about what will happen if I learn you're not being straight with me."

"That's the problem. I'm not straight."

I try to laugh but I can't. Neither can he.

"I'll be in touch."

"You want your hanky back?"

"Would you?"

I open the door, let myself out.

"Let's go, Elvis," I say, making my way back down the corridor toward the county lockup exit. "And no, we don't have time to stop for donuts."

Chapter 37

It's going on ten in the morning by the time find our way out to the Albany County Lockup parking lot.

"Where to now, since we can't get donuts?" Elvis asks.

"State Senator Bates's home."

"Sure we're gonna feel welcome there?"

"Not really."

"Maybe we should get ourselves cleaned up first."

"Not a bad idea, Elvis. Every now and then you come out with something stunning."

"Now who's the bully?"

We make our way through downtown Albany where I make a right onto Broadway, heading south. When I arrive at the entrance to the deserted Port of Albany, I drive across the empty, weed-filled lot to the old warehouses lining the docks where the giant ships used to be moored.

While Elvis showers up, his beefy voice bellowing a water-soaked "Blue Hawaii" loud enough to rattle the twenty-five hundred square foot loft, I crack a morning beer and search the internet for the home address of New York State Senator Jeffery Bates. I'm not even half-way done with my drink before I find the address, which, as it turns out, isn't all that far from Schroder's house. In fact, when I Google Map the location, I can easily see that Bates's house is located less than a mile from the brain surgeon, on the same road, in the same development, same Schuyler Meadow's Country Club golf course butting up against its backyard.

I finish the beer, open another one. Elvis has finished with "Blue Hawaii" and now he's begun "Love Me Tender."

"You're not doing anything funky in my shower, are you, Elvis?" I shout out.

"Very funny, Mr. Moonlight. I can't even see my dick, much less hold it."

Since he's taking so long, I decide to Google Amanda Bates. The web search doesn't reveal a whole lot other than her Facebook page, which has been shut down in the wake of her death. Turns out there are quite a few Amanda Bates's in the world and sifting through every one of them doesn't appeal to me. I go to *The Albany Times Union* to view the obit, which makes her out to be a loving, devoted, sinless daughter and not one who would lure the likes of Stephen Schroder into her bedroom and then cry rape. Just looking at the grainy image of her face, she seems sweet, young, adorable, and innocent. A Lola look alike from a long time ago.

There's an article about Stephen's arrest and his pending conviction of reckless murder, along with a quote by Detective Miller: "If it turns out Schroder is indeed directly responsible for the suicide of Amada Bates, we will stop at nothing to see he is charged to the fullest extent of the law."

Another quote follows his. It's from a law professor at The Albany Law School: "If Stephen Schroder is charged and convicted of reckless murder," he states, "it will set a new precedent for hate crimes perpetrated via social media. This isn't the first time a child has committed suicide because of humiliating second and third party Facebook postings, but perhaps it will be the first time that one of these second or third party culprits pays the ultimate price for their *offenses*." The article ends with a statement from Senator Bates about how broken his and his wife's hearts are over the sad affair.

And while he refuses to comment on Stephen or his arrest, he claims to be placing his "trust in both the American judicial system and the good Lord above." End of statement.

I close the laptop, take a quick drink of the cold beer. It hits me suddenly that what I'm becoming mixed up in is liable to make some waves in the national news. I can't help but wonder if it could be good for business. Not that a head-case like me will ever get rich being a gumshoe.

I take another drink of beer as the shower finally stops, along with the singing. I'm almost sad to hear it end. I'm looking out the window onto the river, but my eyes are seeing Amanda Bates, and when I see the now dead teenager I can't help but see Lola.

My smartphone is set out on the counter in the kitchen area. I don't know what makes me do it, but I pick it up, dial Lola's memorized cell phone. Heart beating in my mouth, I wait for a connection. But I don't get a connection. At least not with Lola. Instead, I get a computerized message: "The AT&T customer you are trying to reach is not available at this time."

I hang up.

Is the customer not available because she's not alive? Or is she not available because she's blocked my phone number?

Elvis steps out of the bathroom. He's drying his hair while the rest of his white, bulbous body and shriveled purple and pink junk is exposed for all to see. Or, for me to see ,anyway.

"Jesus, Elvis," I bark, "put some clothes on for God's sakes."

He laughs.

"I turn you on, Moonlight?" he laughs.

"I hope not. You leave me any hot water?"

"Not a drop," he says, opening the fridge, grabbing

himself a cold beer. "You got yourself a tiny hot water tank."

Visions of a very alive Lola swimming inside my brain, I head into the steamy bathroom knowing a cold shower might not be a bad idea.

Chapter 38

A half hour later, we're driving back to Schroder's neighborhood in Loudonville, the posh North Albany suburb. We pass by the former brain surgeon's big yellow monstrosity first, not saying a word, barely craning our necks to look at it. I continue driving past brand new custom mansions, with their manicured lawns, and picture perfect landscaping, until I come to a home surrounded by a big black wrought iron fence. The kind of fence that consists of sharp, spear-like shafts implanted vertically in the ground so anyone who attempts to scale it risks impaling themselves in the most sensitive of places.

There's a big metal gate that secures the driveway. It's open, which is fortunate for us since I'm not sure Bates will be in the mood to allow a private investigator working for the Schroders into his life right now, even if the doc decided to pay his respects at the funeral. Better I show up unannounced.

"This place is bigger than Graceland," Elvis comments, as I slowly make my way up the long driveway toward a three-story white colonial. The home's front exterior contains four white pillars that support a pyramidal portico and below it, a long wooden porch. The place looks more at home on a pre-Civil War plantation down south than it does in upstate New York.

As we approach the three-car garage, I can't help but notice the five or six expensive cars occupying both the top of the driveway and the circular turn-around in front of the porch. Most of them finished in black and sporting darkly tinted bullet-proof windows. Senator Bates' secret service maybe. That is, if the law calls for state senators to enjoy the protection of a secret service.

Instead of turning right onto the turn-around, I choose the less visible option and park in front of the garage. I am driving a hearse, after all, and these people just buried their daughter less than twenty-four hours ago.

I kill the engine. Elvis and I get out.

"Let me do the talking," I say.

We take the paved sidewalk around the side of the house to the front porch. We climb the stairs, make our way to the big front door. I press the doorbell. A loud chime sounds. We wait. Soon I can make out footsteps. The door opens. It's a woman. An attractive woman, maybe thirty-five or forty. She's dressed in a tight, black, sleeveless dress. She's got shiny, chocolate colored hair that falls against her shoulders like a wave crashing on a pristine beach, and her wrists support an assortment of silver jewelry, while around her neck she wears a silver angel on a sterling silver chain. The angel rests just above her cleavage. On her feet, black pumps. I try to look for a wedding ring, but I can't seem to shift my gaze away from her big brown eyes. Eyes not that different from Amanda's. Not that different from Lola's, either.

"Can I help you?" she asks, softly.

"Dick," I utter.

"Is that so," she says, a hint of smile forming on her tan face.

I shake my head to clear the cobwebs.

"I'm Dick Moonlight," I say, reaching into my jeans pocket, handing her a business card. "I'm a private detective investigating Amanda's death." Gesturing over my right shoulder. "This is my associate, Mr. Hills."

She looks us both over, forms a frown.

"Do you have some kind of ID?"

I extract my wallet from the interior pocket on my thin leather coat, open it, exposing the laminated PI license.

She nods.

I put the wallet away.

"May we come in?"

"This isn't the best of times," she explains. "The family is very upset."

"I understand that, and I apologize for the intrusion. But if I could get a word with the Senator and Mrs. Bates."

"I'm Mrs. Bates' baby sister. And I can tell you right now, she's not talking to anyone. Especially a private detective."

She's beginning to raise her voice. Not a good sign. Then, someone else enters the room.

"What's this all about, Lisa?"

She turns, taking hold of the angel around her neck with the two fingers on her wedding hand. No ring. Moonlight the lucky dog.

The man standing behind her is imposing. Like six feet four imposing. He's fit and well groomed, his salt and pepper hair slicked back on his head with product. Senator Bates.

"These men are private detectives," Lisa tells him. "They're investigating Amanda's death. Shall I ask them to leave?"

He approaches the door.

"I'm Senator Bates. Now is not the best of time for us."

"Now's the only time, Senator," I say.

"And why is that?"

"I've been to see Stephen Schroder in county lockup."

"And?"

"You might be interested in hearing what he has to say about Amanda and the truth about what happened at the Schroder home last Friday night."

I'm taking a hard line with him, but I have no choice. I leave now, I'll never have another chance to steal a private face to face with him.

He stares at me. Into me.

"Okay," he says. "Please come in."

We enter into a giant vestibule that's something out of *Gone with the Wind* with its massive center hall staircase leading up to the second floor and the crystal chandelier overhead. Somewhere off in another room someone is crying. Mrs. Bates, no doubt.

"Shall I retrieve my sister?" Lisa says to the Senator.

"Let's not bother Kathleen lest we need to," he says.

He places his hand on her shoulder, squeezes it. When he removes it, the tips of his fingers slide down her arm and, at the very last moment, their fingertips touch. When they do, they both lock eyes with me. I shoot them a slight smile. I want to tell them I'm trained to notice these ever so subtle gestures, but I don't. Moonlight the sly.

"This way, Mr. Moonlight," Bates says. "We'll convene in my office."

As we walk, I turn and take one last glance at Lisa. Turns out, she's doing the same. Trying to catch a quick look at my backside.

"Gotcha," I say.

But she turns away and disappears into the depths of the mansion.

Chapter 39

Bates's office is cordoned off by a big six-panel door that slides into the wall. Makes me feel like I'm caught up in a Sherlock Holmes novel. The office itself only adds to the illusion. The walls are covered in cherry paneling. The windows are wide and draped with thick black velvet curtains. There's a fireplace to the left-hand side of the door and two tall-backed leather chairs set in front of it. Placed in between the chairs is a wood table. Set upon the table is an ashtray and beside that a metal stand holding several pipes. Located on the opposite side of the wide room is a big desk. If I had to guess, it's built of the same high quality mahogany as some of dad's higher priced caskets.

"Do I know you?" Bates says, his eyes glued to Elvis.

Elvis smiles.

"I get that a lot," he says with a twitch of his lower lip.

"You're not from around here," Bates observes.

"What was your first clue, sir?"

Bates stands with his hands stuffed into his suit jacket pockets. Elvis hulks before him, gut hanging over his tight jeans, a clean T-shirt bearing the words "Only Beer for Me: I'm the Designated Driver."

After a long moment, Bates works up a smile.

"Different strokes," he says. He gracefully crosses the room, goes around his desk, seats himself in his leather swivel chair.

"Can we get down to business, gentlemen?" he asks. "This is a very difficult time for me."

I step over to his desk, stand behind one of the two leather smoking chairs set before it. Looking up quickly, I spot not one but two security cameras positioned up in the corners of the ceiling. They're aimed at me and at Elvis. Someone's viewing and recording our conversation in real-time.

"First of all, Senator," I say, "I'm truly sorry for your loss. I, too, am a father and I can't imagine how difficult it must be to bury your child. Second, I'd like to thank you for taking the time to speak with me."

He nods, cathedrals his fingers, brings them up to his lips.

"You mentioned having spoken with young Mr. Schroder."

"That I did. He claims he wasn't the one who lured your daughter into his bedroom last Saturday night."

He shakes his head.

"If not him, than whom?"

"Stephen claims it was Amanda who lured him. And when he refused to give her what she wanted, she got undressed thinking maybe that would do the trick. When that didn't work, she started calling him names. Calling him gay, a fag, the usual. As it turns out, young Mr. Schroder is indeed gay and having some trouble dealing with it."

A portion of Bates' desk is set aside for some family snapshots. There's one of he and his wife, back when his hair was black and not so coiffed. The two are dressed to the nines at some formal function, holding one another's hands, happy smiley faces beaming at the camera. Her hair is a deep brown like her sister's, her face a bit rounder, her eyes also dark brown but sparkly, like she's got her whole life to look forward to with the man who holds her hand. Perhaps a man who will one day work his way up to be President of the United States of America. People have dreams. Big dreams.

There are pictures of a baby whom I'm taking for Amanda. A picture of a little girl graduating nursery school, a mortar board cap made of colored construction paper set on her head. She's smiling ear to ear, the dimples in her rosy cheeks making her face even more beautiful. The picture beside it shows a young lady with long smooth chestnut hair and eyes like her mother graduating junior high. The one beside that shows her playing soccer with the Albany Academy for Girls varsity team. The last one must be the most recent. It's her senior high school picture. The same photo that accompanies her obituary. Only this version of the photo is not only in color, it's much more alive. She looks just like her mother does in the first photo, only more beautiful, more filled with hope and optimism, if that's even possible. It's like the life between mother and daughter has come full circle. But now that circle has been broken with the daughter's suicide.

The Senator notices me looking at the pictures.

He says, "You think my little girl is capable of something like that?"

I look at her in the senior picture and I look at him.

"That's not for me to say. But what is for me to say is this: a young man is behind bars and is very likely to be the first person in history to be charged with the reckless murder of a young lady who committed suicide. That happens, they will make an example out of him and put him away forever. Is that something you want to see happen, Senator?"

"You actually believe what comes out of that delinquent's mouth, Mr. Moonlight?"

"I'm not sure what to believe yet, which is why I'm here."

"Then allow me to put it this way. Whose word are you going to take? My late daughter's or a known drug abuser, alcoholic, *Scarface*-obsessed, punk son of a bitch who'd kick his own mother in the crotch if he thought he could get a quick laugh out of it?"

"He's got a point, Moonlight," Elvis chimes in. "That Schroder kid is a real asshole. You said it yourself. And he does think he's *Scarface*. You ask me, he ain't dealin' with reality."

"Oh, thanks for that, Mr. Elvis Tribute Man," I say, shooting him a look.

"If you must know the truth, Moonlight," Bates goes on, "little Mr. Schroder has been stalking my daughter since she was in junior high school. He is also responsible for getting another classmate pregnant. I only know this because girls talk, and Amanda confided in me about it."

Bates is a politician and my gut instinct is not to believe a word he's saying. But he's just lost his daughter and what would be his motivation for lying to me? Just to see someone pay for his daughter's suicide, even if that someone were innocent? That doesn't seem a likely scenario to me. But it doesn't make me feel any better about my having fallen for Schroder's bullshit bait.

"One more question, Senator," I say. "If your daughter hated Stephen so much, why did she attend his party?"

"I never said she hated him. She just didn't want to be his girlfriend. If he managed to lure her up to his room, I'm sure he did so through some sort of trickery."

The room falls silent. Through the sliding door, the faint sounds of sobbing can still be heard.

Bates stands.

"I assume our conversation has come to an end, Moonlight? Because I have a terribly distraught wife I must tend to."

I feel sick to my stomach. Maybe it's the drinking. Maybe it's the lack of sleep. Good sleep. Maybe it's knowing Lola could be out there somewhere. Out there without me. Not wanting me. Or maybe it's believing Stephen's story about being gay and not capable of raping Amanda Bates. Whatever it is that's happening to me, my judgment seems to be more off than it usually is.

"Yes," I say, "we're through. My humblest apologies, Senator Bates. And my condolences."

He comes around the desk, goes to the sliding wood door and opens it. Then he shows us to the front door. Before we leave, I take one more look behind me. Lisa is standing there, at the far side of the vestibule where it opens up onto the living room. Seated on a couch is another woman dressed in black. She's sobbing into a handkerchief. For the briefest of moments, she stops weeping and slowly raises her head to get a look at me. We make eye contact. Until I can't stand it anymore and move away. I shoot Lisa one more look before I open the door and walk out.

Chapter 40

Back in the hearse, I slam the dashboard with my fist.

"I'm so fucking stupid."

"Not really *that* stupid, Moonlight."

I turn to fat Elvis.

"Thanks. That helps a lot."

His eyes go wide.

"Well, I just mean you're smart about some things. Other things not so smart. My two cents, of course."

"Shut up, Elvis."

He brings his fingers to his lips, pretends to zip them shut, just like my second grade teacher Mrs. DeLorenzo used to do when the restless kids started talking too much and I was looking for every opportunity possible to get a look up her miniskirt.

I fire up a cig. Angrily.

"You know what I think, Elvis?"

He just looks at me because his mouth is still pretend zipped.

"I think I got duped by an eighteen-year-old thug who is under the mistaken impression he can manipulate me."

The singer mumbles something through his sealed lips.

"Just use your words, Elvis," I say, taking a hit off the smoke.

"I was gonna say maybe you were too easy on that Schroder kid. He'll say anything to make you think he didn't do it. Especially after you balled your fist in his face."

I nod while turning over the engine. I make a three-point turn in the paved parking area in front of the garage and speed back down the driveway, hoping the electronic gates don't close before I get through them. The gates stay open, but the way I'm feeling right now, I'd like to see Stephen's head impaled on one of those fence spikes.

I gun the hearse back through the pristine suburb, until I turn a tire-screeching right into Schroder's driveway. I get out of the car, leave the door open, the engine running. I go to the front door, pound on the bell. When he doesn't answer the door, I go around the back of the house. Schroder's lying out on a chase lounge. He's wearing a pair of big round sunglasses and nothing else but a skimpy speedo. In one hand he's holding a tall red drink with a stalk of celery sticking out of it. A Bloody Mary. In the other hand, he's got his cell phone pressed to his ear.

Opening the pool gate, I stomp my way over to him. He catches sight of me, goes wide-eyed, sits up straight, whispers something into his phone while eyeing me and then hangs up. He gets up.

"Bruce Willis," he says, his face beaming like a Jack-O-Lantern. "What a pleasant surprise."

I knock his sunglasses off his face, revealing his beady eyes. He spills his drink and the glass goes tumbling to the pavement where it shatters. He stumbles a step backward.

"What the hell are you doing?!" he barks.

"That's for operating on someone while you're drunk," I say.

Then I punch him in the stomach. He doubles over, drops his smartphone to the pavement where it too shatters. I follow up with an upper cut that explodes his bottom lip.

"That's for *Scarface*, may he rot in prison."

He drops to the pavement like a wet sack of rags and bones.

That's when I feel someone grabbing me from behind. It's Elvis.

"Fuck you doing, Moonlight?"

"Get off of me," I say, trying to wrestle myself free. But Elvis is a hell of a lot stronger than he appears.

Schroder manages to get back up on his knees, where he wipes the blood from his mouth.

"You're going to pay for that, Moonlight. You just hit the wrong fucking brain surgeon."

"You hired the wrong private dick, asshole."

He stands, his white belly bulging over his banana hammock like uncooked pizza dough. He's bleeding from his bottom lip and it's dripping down onto a sickly patch of gray black hair located directly in the center of his man boobs.

"This time you're really fired." He's huffing and puffing like the beating I gave him is the most exercise he's gotten in years. "Remove yourself and your imbecile sidekick from my estate before I call the police."

"Who you callin' an imbecile?" Elvis barks. Then, tugging at my arm, "Come on, Moonlight. Let's just leave."

I yank myself out of his grip.

"This isn't over, Schroder. Doesn't matter if I'm being paid or not. I'm going to get to the bottom of what happened to that girl. And if you decide to call the cops, remember, I know all about your little Oxy deal."

"Your word against mine, Bruce, baby." He shoos us away with a backhanded wave while painting a fake, shit eating smile on his bulbous, bleeding face. "Now be gone with thee."

He doesn't have to tell us twice, or thrice.

Chapter 41

I light another smoke as soon as I get back in the car. Backing out of the driveway I ask Elvis if there's a place I can drop him off.

"Ain't we still on the case?" he asks, as I put the shift into drive, give it the gas.

"I need some alone time."

"Well, I guess you can drop me off at the house. My wife will be at work anyways and I know where she keeps the key. Might be nice to get a few hours shut eye in my own bed."

He tells me where his house is located on the way into Albany, and I drop him off at the edge of a driveway that accesses a plastic blue two-story colonial.

"I'll call you later," I tell him, but I'm not sure I mean it now that I can't pay him or justify putting his hours toward his bill.

Then I proceed to drive home. When I get there, I head immediately to my bed, which is situated at the far left of the loft, near the bathroom. In a matter of seconds, I'm out like an empty clip on *Scarface's* lil' friend.

I dream...

I'm walking in the cemetery.

It's daytime, with the sun's rays beaming through the breaks in the leaves on the trees. I don't know how I've arrived here. I'm just here. The narrow road is gravel covered and winding. On either side of me are small green hills, each of them dotted with gray headstones. Lurking above the headstones are the trees. Thick, old oak trees, covered in green leaves so that the sun doesn't shine through them so much as pokes holes in them.

She appears as a silhouette off in the distance. All I can make out is the dark shape of a woman as she approaches me along the road. After a few moments, she takes on more detail, and the darkness of her image gives way not just to a woman, but a young woman. It's Amanda Bates. Her dark hair is draping her tan, healthy face. Her eyes are beaming, her lips pressed gently together to form a content smile. She's wearing a flowery dress but her feet are bear. She has her arms held out for me like she wants to hold me.

I go to her, take hold of her hands. It's then I make out the wound on her neck. A thick, purple and black horizontal bruise formed by the rope she hung herself with in the basement of her home...

The dream shifts...

I'm lying on my back. There's a bright light shining in my eyes from a ceiling-mounted surgical lamp. I'm not liking this, so I try and get up from the table. But I can't. My torso, legs, and arms are strapped down tightly. Standing over me are two squat, portly figures dressed in surgical scrubs. One on the left and one on the right. Green masks cover their faces and black-tinted translucent masks cover their eyes. When the one on the left slides his mask down, I can see it's Dr. Schroder. He's wearing that clown-like smile, his eyes narrow and black behind the shield.

"Don't worry, Bruce Willis," he says, in his pseudo-soothing voice. "After I make the initial cuts, you won't feel a thing."

"That's right, Dad," the one on the left says, tugging down his mask and sucking on a lit cigarette. "The brain doesn't feel shit once the skull cap is sawed off. 'Course the sawing hurts like a motherfucker, but it'll be fun to watch Moonlight squirm."

"Oh, yes it will, son. Let's gaze upon Moonlight squirming and writhing, shall we?"

In between puffs of his cigarette, Stephen is taking hits off a can of Heineken beer. Gripped in Dr. Schroder's hand is a stainless steel surgical saw. The circular blade attached to it is maybe eight inches in diameter and ridged with razor sharp teeth. The saw's surface glistens in the light from the surgical lamp. He brings the saw to within inches of my eyes and flicks it on, the rapidly spinning blade buzzing loudly, violently.

They're right. I'm squirming, writhing.

"Easy now, Bruce," he says. "This will pinch a little."

I try to scream, but I can't. It's impossible for me to make even a hint of a sound. I'm paralyzed from head to toe.

"Now then," Dr. Schroder says, "it's time we dig that bullet out of your brain."

He revs the saw, brings it slowly to my forehead, and pushes the blade into the skin and bone...

The dream shifts again...

I'm still lying down, but I'm no longer strapped to a surgical table, two sadistic psychopaths about to saw my skull open. I'm lying in my bed, at home. I'm at peace. Other than the gentle sounds of the Hudson River lapping up against the empty docks outside the walls of this old brick building, the room is silent. When she walks into the dark loft and approaches the bed, I'm not the least bit startled. I can't see her face entirely, but I know it's her. I can smell her rose petal scent, and I can see the outline of her lush long hair as it gently rests against her shoulders. I see her shapely body, her round breasts, heart-shaped hips and bottom. She takes hold of my hand, squeezes it.

"I thought you were dead," I say, feeling tears fall down my cheek.

"Surprise," Lola says, "I'm still here."
She presses her hand against my face, dries my tears...
When I wake up there's a woman sitting on the side of the bed, her heart-shaped backside pressed up against me. I want to believe it's Lola. That what I saw in the dream was real. But it isn't Lola.

It's Lisa, Senator Bates's sister-in-law.

I can't say I'm startled, but her presence provides me with an unexpected jolt.

"I apologize for waking you," she says, softly, turning to face me full on. She's still wearing the sleek black dress from before, and the pumps on her feet. Outside the floor to ceiling windows, the night has already settled in. I've been asleep for hours. "You were dreaming," she adds.

I sit up.

"How'd you get in here?"

She gestures toward the door, doesn't move off my bed.

"It was wide open. You must have been pretty tired. Or pretty drunk. Oh, and there's some blood on your right hand."

"Haven't been sleeping well lately," I say, glancing down at the blood on my knuckles. Schroder's blood. "What brings you here?"

She brushes back her hair, sets it behind her ear. Her eyes are dark and deep, her lips thick and soft. If she weren't up close and personal, I might truly mistake her for Lola, or her niece, Amanda.

"I think you know," says the sister-in-law of Senator Jeffery Bates.

That's when it hits me. Schroder, yesterday, speaking about being in love with a woman whose brother-in-law is a senator.

"How's Doc Schroder feeling?" I say. "Word on the streets is he's in love with you. By the looks of it,

Senator Bates is too. I assume his wife—your big sister—has no idea."

"The doctor will be fine. His lip will be swollen for a bit. As for the two men who are hopelessly in love with me, I think that would be stretching it a bit. I'm not the committal type and, like you've pointed out, Senator Bates is married to my big sister—whom I love very much."

"You maintain your morals," I say. "I like that in a woman. And now you're here to speak with me in private about Amanda."

"Yes," she nods. "Amanda, the poor dear soul."

"And what is it you need to tell me behind the backs of both Schroder and Bates?"

"This thing that happened, between she and Stephen. You should know it wasn't entirely the boy's fault. But it also wasn't entirely her fault either."

I feel her words like a shot to the gut.

"I walked out of your brother-in-law's house convinced Stephen tricked me into thinking he was not only innocent of her suicide, but that he was the victim."

Now she's shaking her head.

"You're not far off. It's true, he's not innocent in the matter, but then, neither is Amanda."

"Explain," I say, sitting up straighter.

"Amanda and Stephen had had their run-ins before. Certainly they'd slept together. Certainly they'd done drugs together. Gotten drunk."

"Amanda and *Stephen*."

In my mind, I'm picturing punching Dr. Schroder in the mouth. A punch meant for his son. I see the blood on my knuckles to prove it.

Exhaling for effect, she says, "I spoke with some of Amanda's friends at the funeral. A couple of them were at the party that night. They saw Amanda and Stephen disappear together up to his bedroom. Disappear together as in mutually agreeing to head upstairs. Later on, though, they were heard fighting."

"Over what?"

"I don't know," she says, withdrawing a slip of paper from out of her bra. "You'll have to ask them."

She hands me the paper. I stare at it. Two names are written in blue ball-point.

Jill Marsh and Kevin Woods. Each of the names have a cell phone number written beneath it.

"Thanks for this," I say, clearing the sleep from my throat. "I'll contact them."

"Can I ask you something?"

"Sure."

"You working for the police?"

"I work for me first, the cops second. Or secondarily, anyway."

She gets up, her hand brushing up against mine, like it had the Senator earlier this morning.

"You're leaving?" I ask.

"My work here is done." She smiles, slyly.

"You sure about that? You could have easily called or emailed me with this information."

Gently she sits back down on the bed.

"Snagged," she whispers.

"You're a bad lady, Lisa," I say. "Bad, but good, too."

"You and me," she says, "we're a pair."

Leaning into me, she kisses me on the mouth.

Our work here is most definitely not done.

Chapter 42

I'm back to staring down at the slip of paper after Lisa is gone. I decide to call the girl first, sensing she would be the most likely to answer a phone displaying a number she doesn't recognize, whereas a guy might choose to ignore it. That is, if my built-in shit detector serves me right, which it most definitely has *not* been doing as of late. Turns out she answers after the second ring.

"This is Jill," she says happily, giddy almost.

I tell her who I am and what I do for a living.

"Oh my God, like, really? I've never met a real private detective before. I thought you guys only existed in mystery novels."

"We're real flesh and blood," I assure her. "Where can we meet?"

"I'm working at the Starbucks in Newton Plaza until eleven. If you wanna come by now, I can take my break early."

"Great. They have beer at Starbucks?"

"No, silly. Just hardcore java."

"Hardcore java just might be the thing I need to wake myself up."

"Oh, sweet. I like you already, Mr. Moonlight."

"Just Moonlight is fine."

"See ya later, tater...I mean, Moonlight."

She hangs up sounding very excited about our coffee date.

Chapter 43

The Starbucks is located in one of those suburban strip malls that began dotting the landscape in the early 1980s, and houses every type and manner of overpriced fast food chains, frozen yogurt shops, hair salons, and coffee houses. I park the hearse in front of the store, causing a few of the college kids who are drinking Frappuccino's out on the deck to do a double-take.

"Anyone want a ride?" I say, as I walk past them to the front entry in my black leather coat and combat boots.

"I'm only taking one ride in one of those, and that ain't happening for a long time," answers a white kid who's as big as a pro football player.

"Pays to be a realist, big fella," I say, as I swing open the door, step inside, gaze upon the service counter.

A couple women are tending the counter. The first one is a young, peppy, blonde, and smallish. The second one is a redhead, slightly overweight and definitely in her forties. My guess Jill is the first girl.

I step over to the counter.

"Jill?" I inquire.

"Moonlight," she beams. Then, to her co-worker. "Suze, I'm going on break."

"You want a coffee?" Suze says to me.

I glance up at the menu board and the one million ways coffee can be served and the many more millions of dollars you can spend for the privilege of drinking that coffee.

"Small, black, no sugar."

"You serious?" Suze says, brushing back red hair behind her ears. "That's it?"

"Yup."

"Here we refer to a small as a 'tall'," Jill chimes in with her rehearsed corporate smile.

"Why? Doesn't seem right."

"Starbucks' marketing strategy," she explains while removing her green apron, laying it over a chair back. "We wish to accentuate the positive. Small sounds bad, but tall sounds nice."

My coffee arrives not in a tall paper cup at all, but a small green cup. Small is small no matter what you call it.

"Three-fifty," Suze says.

"You're kidding. I can buy a can of Maxwell House for only three."

"So go buy a can of Maxwell House and drink it until it's coming out your ears. I don't set the prices."

"You only enforce them," I say, handing her a five. "If a short coffee is a tall, is extortion the price of doing business? Maybe they should call the place Star-Mega-Bucks."

She takes the money, opens the drawer, makes the change. She hesitates then, holding the one dollar bill and two quarters in her hand.

I hold out my hand to take the change.

She makes a head cocking gesture toward a mason jar sitting out on the counter. A pink Post-it note stuck to the jar reads, "College Fund." Someone has sketched a round smiley face beside the two words.

"You look a little old for college, Suze," I say.

"Hey, the student loans are still killing me."

"I get a receipt?"

"Really? I'm busy."

I take a quick look around. There's no one else in the store.

"Forget I mentioned it," I say, taking hold of my tall/short coffee. "I would be honored if you kept the change."

"Thanks so much," she says, dropping it into the jar.

"I'll go grab a tall table," I say to Jill, turning away from the counter, and heading into the seating area.

A minute later, Jill arrives carrying her own coffee. A big coffee.

"What size do you call that?" sipping my hot "tall" but oh-so-small coffee.

"Grande," she says. "Actually, it's a decaf mocha Frappuccino."

"You can say that again."

She starts to repeat it.

"I take that back," I interject.

"It's yummy," she says, taking a sip. When she comes up for air, she adds, "By the way, don't mind, Suze. She's old and she gets grumpy at night. Especially on a Saturday night. She used to live in the 'burbs, but her dentist husband left her for a younger woman. Now she lives in an apartment and has to work here to make ends meet."

"Old? Whaddaya mean old?"

"She's like forty."

"Wow, I'm surprised she can still stand up," I say, shaking my head. "I'll come in more often and lay down five bucks for a shot of coffee. I adore elderly people."

She smiles, like she thinks I'm serious.

"So what is it you wanted to see me about?" she asks.

"You don't already know?"

She makes a frown, brushes back her smooth long blonde hair.

"Amanda and Stephen."

"Right on."

"Amanda's Aunt Lisa told me a private detective would want to speak with me about the...ahhh...tragedy. But I wasn't sure if I should believe her or not."

"After all, private eyes exist only in novels."

She smiles. "Of course, silly." Then, "To be honest, Lisa is a little f'd up. She drinks a lot. Sleeps around a lot, too. I think she's got something going with Senator Bates *and* Doctor Schroder."

"You don't say," I whisper. If only she knew how I chose to while away the past hour with Lisa inside my loft.

"But it is her body," Jill adds. "The woman can do what she pleases with it."

I love the youth of the world. So optimistically liberated. I take a second sip of my coffee. It's almost gone. If my calculations are correct, a Starbucks Tall coffee costs around a buck fifty per sip.

"You were in attendance at the Schroder party the other night?"

"Yup. It was a wild one. Most of our parties don't involve alcohol since none of us are twenty-one. But the Schroders always have beer and liquor, and..." She hesitates, like she just caught herself about to admit to something she shouldn't. She drinks some more Frappuccino. For courage. "Can you keep a secret, Moonlight?"

"Do I look like I can keep a secret?"

"You look more like a dude from an old *Sopranos* rerun than someone who can be trusted with a secret," Jill giggles. "But you're awfully cute for an old guy."

I feel myself blush.

A glance at my transparent reflection in the glass façade reveals a scruffy face, a near shaved head boasting a scar from my botched suicide. Same old black leather coat over a brown work-shirt, tight Levi's, and worn-in combat boots that date back to my stint in the First Gulf War.

"I prefer to think of myself as *Scarface*," I say. "You know, like Al Pacino."

She makes a face like someone dumped vinegar in her Frappuccino.

"Gross. Stephen is like obsessed with that movie. That's real gangster stuff. *Sopranos* are cooler. Or *Breaking Bad*."

"Maybe we should read more books instead of gluing ourselves to the boob high-definition wall-mounted tube. So tell me about the Schroder's house and the secret it possesses?"

"The Schroders always have drugs at their house," she adds, under her breath.

"What kinds of drugs?"

"Mostly pharmaceutical stuff. Stuff the doctor can get from the hospital."

"You don't say. They wouldn't happen to have any Oxy would they?"

She brightens up.

"Stephen and Amanda were soooo into their Oxy. To be more honest, Stephen was dealing it, right at school. He moved Oxy at the boy's school *and* the girl's school. It was easy because the boys can take classes at our school and we can take classes at their school."

"That explains a lot. His numerous suspensions. Were he and Amanda doing Oxy that night?"

"And some other stuff. They went up to his room to smoke and to have sex."

"So they were boyfriend and girlfriend?"

"No, not really. Amanda was just getting off a relationship and she wanted to make her ex jealous."

"Her ex was there?"

"Of course he was. But once Amanda and Stephen

were upstairs, they got into a fight over something. You could hear them yelling. They say he raped her then, but I don't believe any of that for a second. Amanda would have kicked the shit out of Stephen, he was so drunk and high. My guess is they got naked and she passed out for a little while. He picked up his phone and snapped pictures of her while she was out. He was stupid and put them up on Facebook. By the time she found out about it a few hours later, she was coming down from her Oxy high, and feeling low as all hell. The shock and the shame of seeing herself exposed like that for the entire student body of both high schools to see was too much. Now the rest is, well, history, I guess."

I down the rest of my coffee. Make that two dollars a sip. I stand.

"You should know, Moonlight," she goes on, "that when you come down from Oxy it can make you very depressed. Amanda was very up and even more down. She was a sweetheart and we all loved her, but she was getting in too deep with a guy like Stephen and his endless Oxy supply, and we knew it." She tears up. "If only we could have saved her."

"Maybe there was no saving her."

She looks at her watch, stands.

"My break's over," she says, rather sadly.

"You understand, Jill, you might have to tell the police what you told me."

She tilts her head, nods.

"Sure," she sighs. "It's okay. Lisa already told me that, so I knew what to expect."

I see myself making love to Lisa on my bed. My guess is that her coming to me tonight had more to do with wanting to do the right thing than the need for sex with Dick Moonlight, as hard as that concept is to believe.

I hold out my hand. She takes it into her gentle, bird-like hand.

"I'll be seeing you," I say. Then, tossing a wave toward the counter. "So long, Suze."

"Come on back, big tipper," she smiles.

"You can bank on it," I say, turning for the door.

Chapter 44

Back behind the wheel, I retrieve the second slip of paper Lisa gave me, and find the number for Kevin Woods. I punch the number into my cell, wait for a pick up. It never comes. Instead, I get Kevin's prerecorded voice: "Yo, this is Kevin. You know what to do."

"Yes, Kevin," I whisper at the phone. "I do know what the hell to do."

After the beep, I leave my name, the reason for my call, and the number where he can reach me, which is the same number he can plainly see on his caller ID readout. I hang up, giving the possibility of a call-back a fifty-fifty shot.

I fire up the hearse.

I back up, put it in drive, and slowly make my way to the main road. That's when I notice a pair of headlights shining bright in my rearview. Maybe I'm being paranoid, but there's a difference between the casual driver who's simply tailgating me, and someone like the jerk who is entirely up my ass right now. It's not the high-beams he's projecting into the hearse, forcing me to readjust the rearview mirror, that's got me worked up. It's not even the fact the distance between his front grill and my back bumper can't be more than six inches apart. What's got my panties in a tizzy has far more to do with the model and make of his car. It's an old model Cadillac like the one I saw last night in the parking lot of the St. Pius Church.

The Russians are back.

I turn onto the road, come almost immediately to a red stop light. Hit the brakes.

The big Russian behind the Cadillac steering wheel, Hector, slams on his breaks so hard I can make out the squeal of his heavy white sidewalls while preparing myself for the inevitable rear end collision.

But the collision never comes.

He revs the big eight cylinder, his big block head appearing in my side-view mirror, face wide-eyed and angry, the collar on his tracksuit raised high. I gaze into the adjusted rearview to try and get a look at his smaller partner, Vadim. He's enveloped in dark shadow, but that doesn't prevent me from noticing the pint bottle he's stealing frequent sips from, and the lit cigarette he's sucking down.

The light goes green.

Hector hits the horn.

The explosion of the horn nearly sends me through the roof of the hearse.

I drive, lightly tapping the gas so I'm staying ten miles per hour under the forty-mile speed limit. That should chap Hector's ass. The way I figure it, I have two choices. I can either pull over to the side of the road, knowing they will also pull over, get out of the Caddy, approach me on foot, guns in hand, their nervous systems jacked up on Oxy, booze, and who the fuck knows what else. Or I can put the pedal to the metal on Dad's hearse and, for now anyway, try and outrun them.

One more glance in the side-view and another in the rearview.

I see Hector pop a pill, swallow it with a slug off of Vadim's pint. I also see Vadim toss what's left of his burning cig out the window. That's when he uses his now free hand to take hold of something else. Something long, hard, and deadly. A high caliber pistol. A .44 caliber Magnum, to be precise. The same one Hector pointed at my face outside Schroder's office and dry fired. My guess is that this time the hand cannon won't dry fire.

What were formerly two choices is now one.

I bring my booted foot down on the gas.

Hard.

Chapter 45

I've been chased before. Been chased by men in cars who are bent on killing me. And I've been chased by men in cars who merely want to scare me. Harass me. Show me who's boss. It's an intimidation tactic going back to the times of the chariots and the lands of the Pharaohs, when one bad Egyptian guy driving his chariot might chase down a good Egyptian guy in his chariot, and the inevitable fire that was exchanged was not from my friends Smith & Wesson, but from their slings and arrows.

It's possible these Russian goons aren't trying to kill me. Not yet anyway. It's possible they fall into the latter category of wanting to scare me. I have no doubt Schroder called on them to do something before I blow their cover to the cops. No doubt they want to see me change my mind about investigating anything to do with their Oxy business partner.

The speedometer on the hearse hits sixty as I slip my .38 from out of its shoulder holster, thumb the safety off, set it between my legs. Directly up ahead at the end of the south-bound suburban Route 9 is the entrance to West-bound Highway 90. I'm coming up on the back of a family van, its tailgate so close I can easily make out the stick figure Dad-Mom-Boy-Girl-and-Family Dog sticker attached to the glass. I swing the wheel to the left, steer into oncoming traffic, the headlights from a car heading directly for me, blinding me.

The driver of the van now on my right wisely hits his brakes.

Good move, family man.

I swerve around the van, turn the wheel sharply to the right, and get back onto my side of the road.

I check the rearview. Hector hasn't been so lucky. He's stuck behind the van. But as soon as the oncoming traffic is past, he swerves back out into the opposite lane, guns the Caddy's engine. He catches up to me, even with my foot pancaking the gas pedal. The window comes down. Vadim is staring at me, smiling. He raises up the Magnum, kisses the barrel, poises it out the window, plants a bead on my face.

I jam the brakes just as the blast from the hand cannon lights up the late spring night like heat lightening.

Correction: the Russians *are* trying to kill me.

Hector stomps on his brakes, which allows me to juke around him and speed toward the highway on-ramp. I hit the ramp doing eighty, the casket end of the hearse fishtailing as I negotiate the ramp's circular curve, toe-tapping the brakes the entire way or else risk going over the side and flipping in the process.

In no time the Russians are on my tail again. Vadim's holding the gun out the window. He's firing at will, the bullets whizzing past my open driver's side window.

I hit the highway and gun it, cutting off an eighteen-wheeler. The driver lays on the horn, flicks his high-beams on and off. But I'm already gone. I see the Caddy slip into traffic behind the semi. For a time it's hidden from me as Hector tries to pull around the big truck by passing it on its right side.

Bad idea.

Passing a semi on the right can mean a sure death sentence if the operator decides to shift lanes and you're caught in his blind spot. Just the thought of it makes me smile. I slam the brakes, the hearse coming to a full stop. The semi is barreling for me, coming up on me so fast in the middle lane I know the operator has two choices. Go right or go left. I'm hugging the left lane just enough so that I'm banking on his going right.

He does it. He goes right.

I hit the gas. The tires burn rubber as the semi passes, horns blaring.

As I pick up speed, I steal a glance out the passenger side mirror.

The Russians are fucked. The semi cut them off, maybe even side-swiped them. They're stopped, off the side of the road, the Caddy having spun out so that its back end faces forward. I move into the right lane and casually take the exit for Everett Road, which will lead me back into the heart of city.

I'm starting to make out the bright lights of the big city when my smartphone rings.

Chapter 46

"This is Kevin," he says, flatly. "You call me?"

"Hi, Kevin," I say, brightly, my heart still pounding, phone illegally pressed to my ear while I drive. "How are you today?"

"It's night, case you hadn't noticed. And it's none of your business how I'm doing."

"How old are you, Kevin?"

"What are you, some kind of creep?"

"Now, now, Kevin, I'm sure Amanda's Aunt Lisa mentioned I might be calling. She gave me your phone number."

"Okay, what do you want to know?"

"You presently busy, Kevin? Have I caught you in the middle of back to back *SpongeBob SquarePants* episodes or something?"

"I work for a living."

"Well, then, where's a good place to meet up so we can talk, mano-a-mano?"

"Mano-a-mano what?"

"Mano-a-mano. It means hand-to-hand in Spanish but it can also mean, man-to-man, or in this case, man-to-boy."

"I took French in high school."

"That explains it."

"Meet me at Lanie's Bar. You know the place?"

"Yup, I know it. See you in ten minutes?"

"Yeah, ten is good."

He hangs up.

I make a U-turn, head back on into the 'burbs.

Chapter 47

I reach Lanie's Bar at a little after nine. Thus far, the Russians haven't been able to catch up to me. I'd like to keep it that way. But I know eventually they'll find me again. Maybe the next time that happens, I'll have Nick Miller with me, and he can see for himself what kind of dangers the new breed of Russian mobster poses to the free world. Especially my free world.

I kill the engine and return the .38 to my shoulder holster, where it's once more hidden behind my leather coat. I head across the lot to the exterior glass door of the neighborhood gin mill and step inside. The bar is horseshoe-shaped and there's a young woman bartending. She's young and strikingly beautiful, with long, dirty-blonde hair, and blue eyes. She's wearing a black elastic tank top that shows off just enough cleavage to make the middle-aged male patrons stick around for more than one quick beer.

I belly up to the bar, offer her my warmest smile and lay out a ten-dollar bill. She smiles back. Moonlight the irresistible.

"Drink?" she says.

"Budweiser, bottle."

"Easy enough," she says, bending over the cooler to retrieve my beer. When I'm able to peel my eyes off her exposed fleshy areas, I take a quick survey of the few patrons sitting around the bar. One old man on my right whose hands are shaking no matter how tightly he attempts to hold his beer bottle.

To my left stands a man of sixty or more who

appears to be in rock solid shape. He's wearing a T-shirt that says MARINES in big bold black lettering across the front where his pecs fill it out. The T-shirt clings to his muscular arms. He's drinking beer and oblivious to my presence as he obsessively stares at the ceiling-mounted television monitor behind me. When I turn to glance at the monitor, I can see he's playing Power Ball.

No one else occupies the bar.

"Excuse me," I say grabbing the blonde's attention. "Do you know if Kevin is working?"

"Kevin Woods?" she says, brightly. Maybe too brightly. "Sure, can I say who's calling?"

"Dick Moonlight." I take a card from my wallet, hand it to her.

She glances down at it.

"A private detective, huh? Wow, never met one of those before."

I smile. "I get that a lot."

"How exciting," she adds, looking me up and down. "I'll tell Kevin you're here."

"I'd be forever grateful."

"Don't mention it."

She starts making her way back around the bar, and as she does, she issues me a quick parting glance over her right shoulder.

You still got it Moonlight, whatever the hell it is you got...

When she disappears into the back, I steal a sip of my beer. After spending the past twenty minutes being chased by a pair of drugged up Russians bent on putting new holes in my head, the cold, sudsy beer goes down smooth and easy.

Then a slam nearly rocks me out of my combat boots.

"Who's your momma?!" barks the Marine, as he pounds the bar with an iron fist that resembles a sledge hammer.

The old man to my right lights up, lets out a belly laugh.

"Can't hold those goddamned Marines down now, can you, Richie?!" he shouts, his voice old and wavering, but somehow spunky. "I black-jacked the goddamned life savings out of a Marine in Korea, early summer of '53. But he toughed it out and won it back plus my back pay for three months. We went off to fight the goddamned Chinese on Pork Chop Hill a few days later. Never did see the son of a bitch again. Never got his name, either."

I toss him a nod, out of respect. But he just goes back to staring into his beer bottle, those hands trembling, remembering the horrors of Pork Chop Hill.

Blonde Bartender returns. This time she has a young man in tow. He's dressed from top to bottom in a black kitchen staff uniform. He's lanky, with black hair gelled into a faux hawk. He's got a lot of facial hair for his age, and a thick earring in his left lobe that isn't a traditional earring. More like a thick round stone that's been inserted into a gaping hole in the lobe, not unlike something you might see a tribal native wearing in his ear, deep in the Amazon Jungle.

"I'm Kevin," he says.

I hold out my hand.

"Moonlight."

He takes my hand in his, shakes it hard but at the same time, lifelessly.

"Go somewhere to talk?" I say.

"I could use a beer," he says. "You buying?"

"You're a little young for alcohol," I say.

"I'm twenty-one. Twenty-two next month."

"Thought you were in high school?"

"How about we go outside while I have a smoke?" he suggests, before whispering, "Beer," to Blonde

Bartender.

She brings him his beer. "Take it out of here?" she asks, picking up the ten-spot I laid out earlier.

"Wouldn't have it any other way," I say, grabbing my full beer off the bar.

She cashes out the beers, leaves the change on the bar.

Together, Kevin and I head outside. Not quite mano-a-mano, but close enough.

We huddle together at the far end of the building's exterior where a stockade fence has been constructed. The fence surrounds a small seating area dedicated to Lanie's smoking clientele. Kevin knocks out a smoke from a pack of Marlboro reds, offers one up to me. I gladly accept. Stuffing the pack back into his trouser pocket, he pulls out a Bic butane, fires mine up first before firing up his own. What Kevin's lacking in personality, he's making up for in manners.

"My high school career at the prestigious Albany Academy for Boys got cut short while I went down river for a while. Coxsackie Correctional."

"Not the nicest of prisons," I say, taking a drag on the cigarette, exhaling blue smoke into the cool night air. Over the course of my law enforcement career, both public and private, I'd known of at least three different inmates who were shivved to their untimely deaths inside the concrete and razor-wire walls of the Catskill, New York, medium security joint. Anyone who's got it in their skull that medium security is less dangerous than maximum security had better think twice. Medium security simply means you're doing a medium length sentence, like four or five years. Doesn't mean the criminals you're locked up with are any less dangerous than an iron house that holds inmates for life.

"I got involved in a drug smuggling scheme," Kevin says, staring not at me, but up at the stars as if he appreciates the celestial view from outside the joint. And who the hell can blame him? "We were pushing all sorts of chemicals," he goes on. "Pharmaceuticals, mostly. Stuff my partner had easy access to. We made beaucoup bucks in my high school alone."

There's the P word again. Pharmaceuticals.

"Let me guess," I say. "Your partner was Stephen."

"Brilliant," he says. "But it doesn't take a Sherlock to figure that one out."

"How long did you work with him?"

"He was a freshman when I was introduced to him. I was a senior. By then he'd been selling for a long time." He peels his eyes away from the sky, focuses his attention on my face. "Rumor had it his dad introduced him to the business."

I smoke.

"His dad is a brain surgeon. Why would he need to push dope?"

Kevin smokes, shrugs his shoulders.

"Beats the living shit out of me, Mr. Moonlight. Why does anyone start selling drugs?"

"Money. Or, the lack of it. Need I go on?"

"Not really."

"So what happened? How did you end up in jail and not Stephen?"

"We were scheduled to make a drop one night four years ago. It wasn't the usual deal-out-of-your-locker-in-the-basement kind of thing where half the fucking faculty was buying from me. This one took place outside a car wash on Central Avenue. The big one."

"The Hollywood Car Wash?"

"That's it. I was to park around the back, away from the entrance where people pay for their car washes, before driving up onto the automatic rollers. Stephen was going to meet me there. But somebody else met me instead."

"Who?"

"The fucking APD."

"They were waiting for you?"

"Yes, sir, led by a narcotics detective by the name of Nick Miller."

Lightening could have struck and it wouldn't have phased me as much as what the kid just told me.

"I see," I say. "And you still keep in touch with Stephen? I understand you were at his party last Friday night."

"I was."

"You still friends?"

"Let's just say I'm biding my time, and being civil."

"Biding your time," I say. "For what?"

"Never mind for what," he says. "You see, in the beginning, there was never any proof Stephen set me up. In fact, I'm told his dad did his best to see I got the best lawyer in town and that I never wanted for anything while I was in the joint. They indicted me as an adult and wanted to put me away for twenty years in Green Haven, but Doctor Schroder's lawyers copped a plea. I was to do four years in Coxsackie. Three, if I showed good behavior. I got out in three and a half."

"What happened?"

"Someone came after me with a screwdriver after chow. But I was quicker than him. I snagged it out of his hand and stabbed him in the ear canal."

I wonder if Kevin can see how wide my eyes just got.

"Remind me not to piss you off, Kevin," I say. Stealing a drag off the smoke, I take a moment to think. "Is it possible the bust was truly a setup?"

He nods.

"It's crossed my mind more than a few times since I got out. Correction, ever since that animal came after me outside the chow hall."

He gives me this look with those dark eyes that feels like someone filled my spine up with ice water.

"The Schroder's are nasty people," I say. "Sounds to me like you were set up by them to take a fall meant for Stephen. Instead, they gave you up. Then they might have tried to take you out while you were in the joint. I've seen it happen a thousand times before."

He finishes his smoke, drops the butt to the pavement, stamps it out.

"I gotta get back to work," he says, his face ashen in the moonlight.

He pushes past me.

"Kevin," I say. "One more thing."

He turns back to me. "What is it?"

"During the party the other night. Did Stephen and Amanda willingly go upstairs to his bedroom together? Or did he force or coerce her in any way?"

He shakes his head, smiles. But it's not a happy smile.

"You gotta ask? She was as much trouble as he is. The two of them...they were a pair."

"Did you know her well?"

"Fuck yeah, Moonlight. She was my goddamned girlfriend. Until pretty recently."

"So you're the one," I say. "I spoke with a friend of yours, Jill, a little while ago. She said Amanda went upstairs that night with Stephen to make you jealous."

He bites down so hard on his bottom lip I think it might bleed. Thank Christ he's not holding a screwdriver in his hand.

I picture Stephen Schroder in his orange county lockup jumpsuit. Think about the shackles and cuffs on his wrists and ankles. Think about how protected he is behind all that iron and concrete.

"It's possible Stephen will make bail," I reveal.

He purses his lips, the left corner of his mouth

forming a slight grin.

"One can only hope," he says, before disappearing back into the bar.

There's a ceramic bowl set out on the metal table. It's filled with sand. Dozens of spent butts stick out of it. They look like miniature cancer-stick tombstones. I bury the butt, adding one more tombstone to the collection.

"The Schroders have one hell of a talent for ruining people's lives," I whisper to no one in particular.

Heading back inside the bar, I set down my half-consumed beer, then dig out my credit card and slap it down, eye Blonde Bartender.

"Bourbon," I say. "And make it a double."

Chapter 48

I wake up on my bed to the sound of my ringing cell phone, with no memory of having gone to bed in the first place. Even a relatively small amount of Jack Daniels will do that to a man with damaged gray matter. Rolling over, I take a glance at my watch. Seven in the morning. I miss the long gone days of youth when I'd quite naturally sleep in until eleven after having spent a good portion of the night and early morning drinking Jack and beer.

My head hurts.

I slip out of bed, head into the bathroom, drain my bladder then wash my face, brush my teeth. In the kitchen I down four Advil with an entire eight ounce bottle of room temperature spring water. I glance at my phone and see the call came from Georgie. My heart beat picks up and a pit lodges inside my chest. I know he's got news of Lola. Life or death news. I want to call him back, but I can't. Not yet. I just can't face either possibility.

When the coffee's made, I pour in a dollop of two percent milk and take it out onto the back deck with me. As the morning sun shines down on my face, I begin to feel the blood resuming its slow and steady course through my arteries, veins, and capillaries. I'm fully aware it's time to get back to healthy living again. The running. The lifting. The no smoking. The minimal booze. But then the death face of Lola enters into my head and I want to swallow a deep drink of numbness, shaken not stirred. Add to that, the face of a young girl who committed suicide in her parent's basement and I'd just as soon lock myself up in the hotel room along with Jack Daniels for a few days.

My eyes on the steadily moving Hudson River, I can only wonder why I was so deeply affected by young Kevin Woods having lost his ex-girlfriend to suicide last weekend. Maybe it's the fact he not only lost her to suicide but also to Stephen prior to the suicide. Maybe it has something to do with my having something in common with the young man: my having lost Lola, and now having to deal with the possibility she might be back from the dead. But then, no one comes back from the dead. No one except myself, that is. Only Moonlight rises. Again and again.

In my head, I see the sweet, innocent photo of Amanda, and I realize the more I find out about her, the less I know. About the only thing I do know is how much she resembles a young Lola. I've never seen the Facebook pictures Stephen posted. Perhaps that would shed some light on why she decided to kill herself. The only way I can get access to those now is to place a call to Nick Miller. It's time I called the narc turned homicide detective anyway.

Pouring another cup of coffee, I dial Miller's cell, hoping he'll be up.

He answers after the first ring.

"Up with the chickens?" I say.

"Life is short but the nights are long, Moonlight," he says. By the hollow sound of his voice I can tell he's put me on speaker phone and he's driving. "What's on your mind?"

I give him the short of it. About Schroder firing my

ass after I lost my shit on him, about his drug smuggling/dealing partners in the Russian mob trying to exterminate me on Interstate 90, about my liaison with Bates' sister-in-law, about my meeting with Jill at the Starbucks, and about my second meeting with Kevin at Lanie's Bar. About Doc Schroder facilitating his own son, along with Kevin and the now deceased Amanda Bates, in their own Oxy dealing scheme.

"Exactly the kind of intel I'm looking for," Miller says. "So, Amanda wasn't little Miss Innocent."

"It's possible if not probable she wasn't raped, Nick," I say. "And as much as I despise the pudgy blond *Scarface*, you're holding him on a phony charge."

"That's your opinion. He took those pictures of her."

"I agree, that wasn't cool. But how do you know she didn't let him take them?"

"Maybe she did. Doesn't give him the right to post them on Facebook."

"But does that give a court of law the right to peg him with murder?"

"Apparently not. I still say the kid needs to be locked up."

"I agree, but from what I'm hearing, Amanda was more than complicit in this thing. She was selling Oxy with Stephen. I think her family knew about it. Why else would Amanda's own aunt get me directly in touch with those two kids? I'm sure she doesn't like Stephen any more than we do, but you can't justify one girl's suicide by making someone else go to prison for something he didn't do. Justice doesn't work that way. Shouldn't work that way, anyway."

In the back of my mind, I'm picturing Miller's wife...how dead and hopelessly gone she must have appeared to him on the operating table. Like a great writer once said, *The dead look really dead when they're dead.* Miller has his agenda and it's an emotionally fueled one.

"Well, this conversation is for naught, Moonlight," he says.

I sip my coffee, watch a kingfisher make a nose dive into the river where it snatches a small fish in its sharp beak.

"I'm not reading you, Nick."

"I'm currently on my way to Albany County Lockup. Stephen's made bail."

Talking about the possibility of his bail is one thing, but then hearing it's a reality is quite another.

"What happened?"

"It so happens, my gumshoe friend, you're right on the money. One young woman's suicide does not constitute murder on the part of another in any form. The judge tossed the charge of reckless murder out at the kid's arraignment last evening in county court. He also dropped the rape charges, citing insufficient evidence since no seminal fluid was retrieved from her interior. 'Course there's probably a used condom that got flushed but that's not gonna help matters. In the end, the only thing the kid was pegged with was drunk and disorderly conduct. It's possible there could be some charges pending for him uploading the Facebook pictures, but that would have to do with Internet crime, and that's a Federal issue. I'm on my way to signature his release from county lockup, sad as it sounds."

"What about his father? The Oxy smuggling?"

"To be honest, Moonlight, I've been all over that for a while now. Like you said, Stephen is involved, and that kid Woods was involved. Now we know Amanda could have been involved. Point is, this thing is only beginning to reveal its tangled web of scumbags. Also, I'm sure there's more than just those two Russian clowns in this thing, and as soon as I know more about who and what is involved, I'm gonna bring the whole house down. But it calls for patience."

"So you're saying it's too early to bust the doctor."

"Yup. If we can't get Stephen on reckless murder, we'll get him on dealing pharmaceuticals along with the old man. He won't go away forever, but he'll go away for long enough."

"That is, if the kid lives long enough."

"What's that supposed to mean?"

"Last night when I mentioned the possibility of bail to Woods, he acted kind of strange."

"Like how strange? Like he'll be waiting for him with an axe strange?"

The image of a screwdriver crosses my mind.

"Sort of. Woods shot me this look. Gave me the willies."

He goes quiet for a moment so only the sound of the air rushing by his car fills the line.

Then, "You working for anyone right now, Moonlight?"

"Not exactly," I say.

"Good, meet me at County Lockup. I've got an idea."

"When?"

"Now."

"Now? I'm hung over as all fuck."

"So am I. Doesn't stop me from serving and protecting."

"I'll be right there," I say. "But one question."

"What now?"

"What if the Russians show their faces again?"

"You got a gun, right?"

"Affirmative."

"You got bullets to go with the gun?"

"You gotta ask?"

"So load the gun and use it if you have to. Now, we done here? I gotta stop for coffee."

"The Facebook pics of Amanda. Do you have a copy?"

"You haven't seen them yet?"

"Not sure I want to. But I feel like I need to."

"I've got your email. I'll send them over to you from my smartphone."

"Thanks."

"You won't be thanking me after you see them."

He hangs up.

I head inside for my third cup of coffee while I get dressed.

Chapter 49

Driving, I'm careful to keep a sharp eye out for an old model Cadillac as I take Interstate 90 to the Albany International Airport exit, which is the same exit for the county lockup. Miller is waiting for me in the parking lot, two large Dunkin' Donuts coffees in hand.

"Thought you could use one of these, Richard," he says. "Maybe it's time you think about slowing down on the booze."

"I could inject gasoline into my veins right now and it wouldn't make any difference," I say, taking hold of the coffee. "I was a jerk to you yesterday. My apologies. I promise never to call you Barney Miller again. The similarity is in name only."

Folding back the plastic tab on the cup, I drink some of the hot, black-no-sugar coffee.

"Gee, I think I'm gonna tear up," Miller says. Then, "Raise your right hand."

"What for?"

"Just do as I say."

I do it. I raise my right hand.

"Do you solemnly swear you will uphold the law and position of Deputy of the Albany Police Department, in accordance to the law and requirements of yadda, yadda, something, something, so help you God?"

I look at him. Into his steely gray eyes. I'm not entirely sure why he's doing this, but then, I need a job.

"I do, baby." Then, bright eyed. "Hey, it's better than Barney."

"Cut the shit," he says, reaching into his blazer

pocket, pulling out a leather wallet-like object. "This here's your temporary badge." He hands it to me.

I open the wallet, glance down at the badge. It's identical to the one I once carried for the APD for real. I fold the wallet back up, slip it into the interior pocket of my leather coat. My built-in shit detector speaks to me. I hope I can trust what it's telling me.

"You want me to stand guard over Scarface, don't you?" I intuit.

"APD would never authorize the use of one of our blue uniforms for the job. We're sorely under-staffed as it is."

"Then you agree, his life could be in danger." A question.

He nods.

"If what you tell me is true," he says, "I do. But there's another, more important reason why I'm deputizing you."

I drink some coffee.

"Can't wait to hear it," I say.

"I want you to make good with Doc Schroder. Apologize to him. Then I want you to get everyone in one place. The Doctor, Stephen, the Russians. Video tape the proceedings if you can. Make them talk about their deals and former deals. Make them name names."

"How do I go about getting them to trust me?"

"You're going to tell him you want in on the drug op."

I laugh. It just comes out.

"Me? Schroder will never go for it. I just bloodied his lip and spilled his Bloody Mary."

"If you put up the right amount of investment money, he will. He's going broke, fast."

"How much?"

"My guess is ten grand will do it for the initial buy-in."

"Where do I get that kind of money?"

Just then, a blue and white turns into the lot, its flashers going but the sirens turned off.

"Just in time," Miller says, smiling. "The bank has arrived."

Chapter 50

We stand over the trunk of the blue and white. Miller, myself, and an aviator sunglasses-wearing officer who not only doesn't acknowledge my presence, but ops for not saying a word regarding the proceedings. Using the key, the cop opens the trunk, revealing a plain blue and white duffel bag. The kind of duffel I used as a book bag back when I was a kid. A canvas bag with a flat hard bottom, plastic horseshoe-like handles and a zipper that goes from one end to the other. Miller reaches in, unzips the bag part way, revealing numerous stacks of twenty-dollar bills. He rummages around the bag for a bit, until he's satisfied with what it contains. Then he zips the bag back up, and removes it from the trunk.

"Ten grand," he says. "In marked bills."

"Marked how?"

"A digitally installed GPS traceable watermark not even Alan Greenspan could find, even with one of Obama's NSA spies holding a gun to his head."

"That's what they all say," I say, my eyes peering at the dead-faced cop.

He doesn't laugh.

"I suppose you want me to hand this money over to Doc Schroder."

"That's your buy-in money."

"What if he wants more?"

"Chance we take."

He hands me the bag. It's surprisingly heavy. Maybe it wouldn't be so heavy if it were mine, and not so traceable.

Miller turns to the cop.

"You're dismissed, officer."

Without a word, the cop gets back in the car and takes off.

I head to the hearse, place the money in the back where the caskets used to go. I shut the door, turning back to Miller.

"You sure this is legal?"

"Sure," he says. "Standard sting operation."

"Using me as the bait."

"I wouldn't actually call you bait. More like a stand-in for a real cop. Just in case the lead starts flying."

"Gee, thanks. Nice to be wanted."

"Look at it this way, Moonlight. Your rep with the department sucks. You pull this off, bring the Schroders and their drug dealing buddies down, you'll look like a hero in their eyes."

"Wow, a real hero. Maybe Whoopi Goldberg will have me on *The Vagina*."

"That's *The View*, and who knows, so long as you don't get yourself killed."

"Yes, getting killed would end the hero thing pretty quick. But then, I'd be a martyr."

"Shall we go get that kid out of jail?"

"Would it make a difference if I said no?"

Miller starts walking toward the lockup's front entrance, like my opinion doesn't mean shit.

Chapter 51

Scarface Stephen is psychopathically wired, his eyes bloodshot and piercing. Now that he's ditched his county jumper, he's back to wearing husky skinny jeans that hang half way down his ass, a black T-shirt with a silhouette of Pacino and his gun, topped off with his extra wide-ghetto-brimmed Yankees baseball cap. He looks like exactly what he is: a white-bread, silver-spoon-up-his-fat-ass, suburban dope pusher who's just been liberated from the clink.

"You responsible for springing me?" the kid says as we make our way back across the parking lot with Miller in tow.

"Maybe," I say. It's best for him to think he owes me one.

I stop at the hearse, turn to face the detective and Stephen.

"I don't have to tell you that the APD is watching you, Mr. Schroder," Miller says to the now free kid. "I'm entrusting Moonlight here to escort you home and look after you until things settle down."

"What fucking things?" the kid says, his face bitter and hard, despite its physical softness.

It dawns on me he probably thinks I'm still buying into his *I'm gay and the real victim in this* story, and that obviously the cops have bought into it, too. Which just might work in our favor.

"The judge might have tossed out the count of reckless murder for now, but the prosecuting attorney is still hard at work trying to find a way to nail you for complicity in Amanda's death. Her father is a state senator. Her death made big news. National news. The public is angry at what happened to her. They want revenge. Your life could be in danger as we speak. Mortal danger."

Miller's really laying it on, raising the concept of bad cop to an entirely new level. Without having to be told, I take my cue.

"Hold on just one stinkin' minute, Detective Miller," I insist. "Stephen has been wrongly accused here. The judge proved it when he killed the charges. He's not even the type to go after someone like Amanda. He's a sorely misunderstood young man who's been through a lot and just wants to get back home. Isn't that right, Stephen?"

We both lock eyes on the kid. His chubby, beady-eyed face takes on a new pale glow.

"Yeah, listen to Moonlight, Detective Miller. He might be a bit of a douche bag, but he speaks the truth. I've been railroaded." He brings fisted hands to his face, rubs his eyes with them like he's about to break out in tears. "I'm so, so sensitive. I just want to be liked. I know what my dad did to your old lady. But it's not my fault."

I toss Miller a wink. He winks back, painfully.

"You just get yourself home, young man," the detective says. "Due process of the law will run its course one way or another."

I open the passenger side door for Stephen like I'm his chauffer. He plops himself down on the seat.

"Oh, and one more thing, Stephen," Miller says. "Stay close to home. You're out on bail pending charges for your numerous crimes. Understand?"

"That's quite enough for today, Detective," I say, closing the door. Then, as I walk around the back of the hearse. "How'm I doing?" I say under my breath as I pass within inches of Miller.

"He mentions my wife again I'll shoot him in the head," he says. Then, "The Schroders are gonna be eating off your dinner plate in a matter of moments."

"That would be the plan," I say. "I'll be in touch. Soon."

Miller turns, starts heading back to his ride.

I get in, start the hearse up.

"Let's go home, Stephen," I say, roaring out of the lot.

"Let's head to the nearest liquor store, cock-a-roach," he says. "Today's my birthday and I'm fuckin' thirsty."

Chapter 52

Not one to argue with a psychotic drug dealer, I find a neighborhood liquor store and buy the kid a pint of vodka and a pack of Marlboro reds. While I'm in the store, I place a call to Elvis.

"Thought I'd never hear from you again, Moonlight."

"I'm like a rotten penny," I say. Then I fill him in on what's happening on with Stephen, along with mine and Miller's plan to get back on Doc Schroder's good side.

"You're gonna give him ten grand?"

"That's the idea. And I need you to be Johnny-on-the-spot with a video camera."

"It's not like I can just stand there filming. I'll need equipment. Real spy equipment, like Tom Cruise uses in *Mission Impossible*."

"You got a credit card that works?"

"Yeah. I can steal one from the old lady."

"Go buy what you need. Save the receipts and I'll get you reimbursed from the APD."

"Cool. I get to be a spy. Just like Elvis and Tricky Dick Nixon."

"That's a stretch."

"When do we meet back up?"

"Head back to my loft as soon as you've bought the stuff."

"Roger that, Chief."

"Don't call me Chief."

* * *

Back in the car, Stephen cracks the cap on the bottle, takes a drink that would knock even me out. He lights up a smoke, offers one to me. I take it, set it between my lips unlit.

"Didn't know you smoked, Moonlight," he says, handing me the lighter.

I light up.

"I'm not a smoker. I'm a quitter."

He takes another swig off the bottle.

"How's about a drink?" he says, passing over the bottle.

"Well, seeing as it's your birthday."

I set down the lighter and take hold of the bottle. I drink a half shot, hand it back to him.

"And a boozer to boot," he laughs. "First you help me get out of jail, then you defend me against that sorry ass detective prick, and now you're partying with me. You've grown a whole new skin, Moonlight. Maybe my dad will give you your job back, even though you gave him a fat lip."

"You're going to have to forgive me, Stephen," I lie. "And I'm hoping your dad does, too. I misread things. Misjudged you. I know you could never rape anyone, never cause them to commit suicide. I should have never hit your dad. I'm...I'm...I'm so ashamed."

I make sure there's a tear-jerking crack in my voice when I say "ashamed," just for drama's sake. The kid's buying it hook, line, and fucking sinker.

"I do have one confession, though," the kid says.

"You can trust me," I say, knowing what he's about to say, but playing dumber than dumb.

"I'm not gay. Or, well, let me put it this way. I'm not looking to fuck guys in the ass." He giggles, then pauses to smoke for a minute. "But if I were to ask you to pull over, maybe behind a gas station or something, I would give you the privilege of sucking me off."

Freon runs through my veins. My heart begins to throb in my temples. I have to think quick on this one. No way I'm sucking him off. But then, no way am I about to piss him off, either.

"Gee, Stephen," I say, "I can't tell you how honored I am, you asking me to do that."

"But you're gonna say no, aren't you, cock-a-roach?" he snaps. "Maybe you are still an asshole."

"Hey, hold on, kid," I say, trying to calm him down. "You see, with that little piece of bullet in my brain, I must refrain from any and all sexual activity. Not many people know that secret, but now you do."

"Really," he says "No shit?"

"It's true. The arousal from sexual activity will not only cause me to pass out and enter into a coma, it can result in a serious case of S.I.L."

"What's S.I.L.?"

"Sudden and Irreversible Lockjaw."

"Lockjaw," he repeats as we get onto Highway 90, eastbound toward the suburbs.

"Imagine my jaw clamping irreversibly shut on your manhood while in the process of taking care of it. You'd not only bleed to death, you'd become an entirely different gender."

"Holy crap," he says. "You're right. I could make you give me a hand job, but you're driving. Tell you what. After being locked up for two days with no peace, I got a boner that just won't quit. You're lucky I'm not already jacking off."

Holy fuck, the things I have to do in the name of law and order and righteousness.

"We'll be home in six or seven minutes," I say. "You can take care of yourself then."

I step on it, before the kid decides to relieve himself in front of me.

* * *

Exactly five and a half minutes later, we finally hit his driveway. He jumps out of the car with his half empty bottle of vodka, his new pack of smokes, and his hard-on.

I watch him casually walk the length of the driveway, his pants belted around his thighs, and his oversized *Scarface* T-shirt falling just short of them. I'm trying my best to resist the voice in my head that's telling me to blow the little deviant motherfucker away at my earliest convenience.

Chapter 53

I get out of the hearse, head around to the back of the house. It's a good thing I've learned the value of self-control over the years. Because the way I'm feeling right now, I'd just as soon grab my gun, shoot the entire joint up, then set it ablaze. Goodbye, Schroders. Goodbye any trace you ever existed. Moonlight the totally fucking fed up.

Doc Schroder is standing pretty much in the same place I left him yesterday. Sunning himself by the pool. Only he's not lying down. He's embracing his son, hugging him like he's just returned from the wars. He catches sight of me and releases the kid.

"I don't recall inviting you here, Moonlight!" he barks, his swollen bottom lip butterfly clamped, his beady eyes covered in those thick sunglasses. He's back to wearing nothing but a skimpy Speedo, like it's mid-summer, his white gut protruding like a basketball-sized tumor.

"It's okay, Dad," Stephen says, coming to my rescue. "Turns out, Mr. Moonlight is okay. He helped get me out of jail. He also defended me against that stupid piece of white bread, Detective Miller. You know, the one who thinks you killed his wife."

I slowly make my way into the backyard, the big house's deck to my left and the Olympic-sized swimming pool to my right, the small patch of woods that separate the property from the golf course beyond that. Schroder grows more rigid and afraid the closer I come to him. Like I'm about to beat him up again. But

I'm not. Instead, I do something far different. I hold out my right hand.

He looks down at the hand.

"What the hell am I supposed to do with that?"

"Maybe he'll jerk you off with it," Stephen says, firing up another smoke.

"Stephen!" barks the brain surgeon. "That will be quite enough."

"Yeah, fuck you, too, Pop."

Schroder turns back to me.

"Listen, Doc," I say. "I want to extend my most humble apology to you. I misjudged you. I misjudged Stephen."

"That's what he said to me when he sprung me out of the clink," the kid interjects.

"Please, Doc," I push.

Schroder continues to stare down at the hand.

"Well, you did help get Stephen out of jail," he says. "And I can see where perhaps you might have acquired the wrong idea about us, having witnessed what on the surface might be interpreted as an illegal transaction with my Russian acquaintances."

"Can we be friends again?" I ask, piling it on.

He smiles. A thin, ear to ear smile, like you might see on a fat clown. It gives me a case of the shivers.

He takes hold of my hand with his wet, chubby fish of a hand. We shake, loosely. Then I extract my hand, try not to let him see me when I wipe my palm off on my pant leg.

"However, I'm not sure I want to hire you back, Moonlight," Schroder says, making his way back to the pool, where he resumes his horizontal perch on the chaise lounge. I follow right behind him. He's once more drinking a Bloody Mary with a long celery stalk sticking out of it. The remnants of yesterday's broken Bloody are gone, like the spilled blood at a white-washed crime scene.

"I'm not looking to work as a private detective for you anymore," I say. "My work there is finished, now that Stephen is free." As if on cue, we both catch a glance of the kid as he downs the rest of the vodka pint and smokes his cigarette. He's drunkenly dancing on the deck to a song on his iPod, the wires from the white earphones swaying with his every awkward movement.

Turning back to one another.

"I realize I'm not in a position to ask anything of you, Doctor Schroder," I say, after a beat, "but I'd like to make you a proposition."

He seems a bit startled.

"You propositioning me? Come now, Bruce Willis. And here I thought we were just friends."

I fake laugh.

"Not that kind of proposition," I say, recalling Stephen's offer to blow him on his way home from jail. Like warped father, like warped son. "A financial arrangement, let's call it."

"What exactly did you have in mind?"

"Truth is, Doc, I'm broke. Broker than broke. I've got more bills than cash, no work, and my child support payments are so far behind I'll be lucky not to land in prison by the end of the year."

"My, my. You are in bad fiduciary shape. Worse than myself, perhaps." He giggles, reaches for his drink, takes a long, slow sip. Setting the glass back down, he wipes his thin, bee-lipped mouth with the back of his hand. "What is it you have in mind?"

"I'm not suggesting your arrangement with the Russians isn't anything other than you providing them with a much needed prescription."

"Ha, ha, Moonlight. Just yesterday you accused me of running drugs."

Holding up my hands.

"I know and I apologize for that." Lowering my hands. "However, if it should happen you and the good Russian people are making deals for pharmaceuticals on a larger scale, I was wondering if you wouldn't entertain an investor."

He stares at me through those round sunglasses.

"And if I were to even consider for a minute saying yes to something like this, what would you use for money? And what kind of clientele would you be bringing to the party?"

Over my shoulder, I catch another glance at Stephen. He's still dancing, but now he has a can of beer gripped in his right hand.

"I have five thousand cash," I say. "I might be able to get you another two if I call in some old loans."

"And buyers?"

"I'm fairly certain I can get some part-time night work as a security guard at Albany State. You can imagine the market for Oxy on a campus of seventeen thousand spoiled kids and left-of-center professors?"

"So why not just reduce your overhead and DIY?"

"You control the product. I have zero access to Oxy or anything like it."

"True. Guess you could say I hold the cards. Conceptually speaking, of course."

"I'm quite sure I can help you triple your sales. Maybe even quadruple them."

"That so, Moonlight. This sounds very, very illegal and I am in no way admitting to selling illicit pharmaceuticals. But I'm curious about your proposal. Just listening, is all."

Stephen tosses the empty beer can into the pool where it makes a tinny hollow metallic noise. He jogs into the kitchen to grab another.

"Way I see it, Doc," I say, "I need you, and you could most definitely *use* me and *use* my cash."

"Cash?"

"Cash."

"Ten grand," he says. "No less."

I anticipated his raising the ante, which is why I low-balled him to begin with.

I shake my head.

"Impossible," I say. "But I'll see what I can do."

He stands.

"Remember, Moonlight," he adds, "I really have no idea what you're talking about when it comes to the sale of anything illegal like Oxy. And if it should happen that you're wired right now, or someone is somehow listening in on some sort of high tech device, it should be stated for the record you've approached me and not the other way around."

"I'm not wired," I say, tugging out my shirt tails, unbuttoning my shirt exposing bear skin. "No high tech listening devices."

Reaching out slowly with his right hand, Schroder brings his fingertips to my chest. It creeps me out.

"You have a fine body, Moonlight. If I were a gay man, I'd jump your bones."

I button back up, shove my tails back into my jeans.

"Do we have a deal?"

"I'll call you," he says. "But first, I want something from you."

"Anything," I lie.

"Stand still," he says.

I stand there while he makes a fist, sucker punches me in the gut. Funny thing is, I don't double over. I don't shout out in pain. I don't cry. I merely wince as his powerless punch bounces off my stomach muscles.

He takes a step back, rubs the pain off of the knuckles on his punching hand.

"That didn't hurt?" he asks.

"No," I say.

"I'm impressed."

"I try and stay in shape."

"I can see that, Moonlight," he says, his white puffy face having turned fifty shades of red. "Thanks for bringing my son back home to me on his birthday, Bruce Willis. You're a real superhero."

"Don't mention it."

"Listen, why don't you come by tonight. I'm throwing the lad a birthday party. Eight o'clock. Sound good?"

"Yeah, sounds good," I say, wishing that bullet would shift in my brain so I could die right now, on the spot.

"My Russian friends will be here," he says, making a frown. "Sadly, they have become something of a liability."

"How so, Doc?"

"They drink too much. For certain they do too many drugs. And they can be...how shall I say this?...quite dangerous, especially when given access to firearms." He pauses for a moment, looking off into the distance. Then, "It would be a shame if something bad were to happen to them tonight at the party."

"Something bad?"

He reaches out, pats me on the chest in precisely the spot where my shoulder-holstered .38 rests against my ribcage.

"If they were to be accidentally wounded by someone who really, really, really wants to do business with me. If you get my drift. Because should we do business together, Moonlight, Lord knows it would go a heck of a lot smoother without those two Russian bears in the picture. Plus the take would become much larger for each of us. That is, should you prove yourself worthy of doing business with me."

"I get your point, Doc. You'll let me do business with

you if I assassinate the two Russians for you."

He pats my arm.

"Did I say that? I was just thinking out loud. In any case, I'll see you later. If in the meantime, I decide to accept your offer, I'll call you."

"Thanks," I say, backing away, turning and heading toward the driveway.

I toss a wave to the iPod and booze-soaked Stephen. He's got one of those Super Soakers in his hands. A rifle sized squirt-gun that shoots a powerful spray of water a thousand feet or something. He plants a bead on me with the business-end of the Super Soaker, triggers a blast of water that nails my temple, in the precise spot where a chunk of .22 caliber bullet pierced it once upon a time. At least he didn't tell me to say hello to his *leetle frien*, again.

I ignore him and keep on walking.

Fast.

On my way out of hell on earth.

Chapter 54

As I slip behind the wheel of the hearse, my smartphone chimes.

I glance down at the digital caller ID. It's Georgie again. Here's what I do: I don't answer the phone. I ignore it, start the engine, back out of the driveway.

All the way home, I wonder how I'll handle the news about Lola being alive.

Chapter 55

Back at the loft, Elvis is waiting for me at the kitchen island counter. He's got a bunch of gadgets set out. He's drinking a beer.

"Where's mine?" I say, glancing at the can of Budweiser.

"Bad day that's only gettin' worse?"

"I'm officially back to being Schroder's bitch," I say, opening the fridge, grabbing a cold one. "But thus far, the plan has worked like a charm." I crack open the beer, steal a deep drink, take it with me over to the island counter. Then I proceed to fill Elvis in on my pool-side meeting with the doc, including the little bit about taking out the Russians.

"So Schroder's really gonna let you partner up with him?"

"So long as I prove myself worthy and deliver the cashish." Then, "What's all this stuff?"

"Combo video/still camera, courtesy of my soon to be ex-wife. Zoom lens also courtesy of my soon to be ex-wife, and the piece de resistance, a bionic ear." He points to a pair of black headphones attached to a small black disk that looks identical in both size and shape to the one-thousand-channel television satellite disks most rednecks attach to their double-wide trailers. "Cost the APD four hundred bills, but it will be worth it. It not only eliminates background noise, but it can hone in on a conversation from up to two hundred feet away."

"Good work, Elvis. Next thing I need is for you to grab your Elvis outfit. The 1977 white jumpsuit thing.

I've got a gig for you tonight."

"What's the occasion?"

"Our boy Stephen Schroder's birthday party."

"Not exactly my kind of gig."

"My plan is simple. I'm going to finalize my deal with Schroder for running the Oxy as soon as I arrive. I'm going to lure him into the backyard so it will be a no brainer for you to record the audio-visual for the entire proceedings. Soon as that's done, and we head back into the house, I want you to ring the front doorbell. You'll be Elvis from that point on. Inside your costume, you'll be carrying my .38."

I remove the pistol out of my shoulder holster, set it out onto the counter.

"Why not just carry it in yourself?"

"It's possible Schroder's gonna pat me down. If not him, then maybe the Russian goons will. But even if they don't, I'm thinking that if I'm not carrying heat, Schroder might not make me assassinate Hector and Vadim."

"What if Schroder makes you use one of his own pistols?"

In my mind, I picture the Glock the ex-brain surgeon has stored in the glove compartment of his Beemer.

"He won't want to link his licensed pieces to a double homicide."

"He's probably got some unlicensed pieces for just such an occasion."

"Then so be it. He wants blood on his hands, then it's going to come from one of his own guns. Either way, I think the best policy is to go in there clean as a whistle. Understand?"

He nods.

I look at my watch. It's slightly past noon. Time to call Miller, give him the details of my plan.

"You want I should be waiting nearby with the

cavalry?" he asks. In my head, I see him sitting behind his old wood desk, the ball knot on his tie perfectly tied and positioned.

"Might be nice. But if Schroder thinks for even a split second that he smells a cop, this thing is shot to hell."

"I understand. You're doing your old department a great service, Deputy Moonlight."

"Wow, I feel all warm and tingly inside."

"You're much easier to deal with when you're getting laid regularly."

"I think Amanda's Aunt Lisa was a one shot deal."

"Probably better that way."

He hangs up before I have the chance to tell him I couldn't agree more.

Chapter 56

Maybe entering into the hornet's nest without my .38 is a bad idea, since the doc is going to insist on my becoming a murderer in the name of Schroder loyalty. But I'm not about to leave myself unprotected. In the top drawer of my desk, I locate my spare pistol. It's a small unlicensed .22 caliber snub-nose revolver with the serial number scraped off. The same revolver I used to kill myself. Most people would probably get rid of the weapon they used to try and blow out their brains. That is, if they survived the attempt, like I did. But I like to keep it around for the same reason I like to drive Dad's hearse. It reminds me instant death is always a distinct possibility in my life.

Slipping the pistol into my leather coat pocket, I head back to the island counter, down the rest of my beer. I grab hold of my car keys.

"Where you going, Chief?" Elvis asks.

"We've got a few hours before Schroder's expecting me back at his house. I have some personal business to attend to first."

"Care to let me in on that personal business?"

"No."

I leave the loft, not knowing if I'm about to do the right thing or the wrong thing. But then right or wrong, I'm going to find Lola and I'm going to find her right now.

Dead or alive.

Chapter 57

By the time I get back in the hearse, Georgie has already left me another message. I haven't listened to a single one of them. Eventually I'm going to have to face the truth. Or maybe that bullet in my brain will shift right now and someone...probably fat Elvis...will discover my body in a few hours, the rigor mortis having already kicked in.

I decide not to bother with leaving a message. I opt for calling him in real time.

"Jesus, Moon," he barks. "Where the fuck you been? I thought you might be dead."

"By the Grace of God I go."

"Ain't that the goddamned truth."

"Such language."

"I have some fucking news."

"Good news?" I say, my stomach cramping up, my throat constricting, my head ringing like a bell.

"Depends on how you look at it. Meet me at McGeary's Tavern in fifteen minutes. I'm buying."

"I'll be there. May God strike me dead."

Chapter 58

Georgie is already there when I walk into the bar. McGeary's is one of those old time Albany bars that's been in existence since the city itself. It's a long, cavernous bar, set inside an old downtown brownstone facing the Hudson River. The floor is old black and white marble tiles, and the ceiling is ornate hand-crafted tin painted white. The walls are finished with wood paneling covered in mirrors along with framed black and white photos of old Albany and some other cool stuff, like former New York State Governor Rockefeller flipping the bird at some reporters. There's even a big, full-color, 1972 re-election poster of Nixon that's been hung upside down.

Georgie occupies the far corner seat closest to the river. He's dressed in blue jeans with tears in them, and his favorite pair of cowboy boots. His long silver hair is pulled back into a ponytail. He's sipping on a Coors Light while chatting it up with Tess, McGeary's owner. Tess is a red haired beauty with an ample chest that fills out her red-velvet gown. Green eyes and luscious lips, she is an Albany legend, and I've had a major crush on her for years. If only she weren't batting for the other team.

I ignore Georgie and, instead, lean over the bar and plant a fat one on Tess.

"Hello, beautiful," I say.

"You look like shit, Moon," she says with her characteristic smile. "Maybe I should cut you off before you start."

"I've already started," I confess.

"In that case," she says, popping the top on a tall-necked bottle of Budweiser beer, setting it onto a coaster before me. "But no Jack."

"We'll see about that," Georgie says.

Tess slides down the bar to tend to a construction worker who's just entered into the establishment and taken a stool further down from us. I turn to Georgie.

"Let's have it," I say.

Georgie wraps both hands around his beer bottle, but he doesn't drink.

My beer sits on the bar. I'm too weak, or perhaps too paralyzed with fear, to raise my hand to drink from it.

"I'm not sure how to say this, Richard," he says, while exhaling a breath. "So I'm just gonna say it. She's alive. Lola. Is. Alive."

Chapter 59

The life drains from my head like the last bit of soapy water down the shower drain. For a brief few seconds I see bright white lights flashing behind my eyeballs. I begin to sway on the bar stool, but Georgie catches me before I enter into full pass-out mode.

"You okay, Moon?" he says. "We can go in back, into the dining room. You can lie down in an empty booth."

I look for Tess out the corner of my left eye. Luckily, she hasn't noticed my dizzy spell, thanks to Georgie's quick thinking. He takes hold of my beer, aims the neck at my mouth.

"Here," he insists. "Drink this. Doctor's orders."

As mandated, I drink. Half the bottle. Maybe I should be drinking water instead but somehow the cold effervescent beer does the trick. Within moments, I'm feeling better, stronger. Strong and balanced enough not to fall off the bar stool, anyway.

"How do you know?" I say. "How do you know she's alive?"

"I checked with downstate. Newburgh General, which was the closest medical center to the highway accident."

In my head, the events of that sunny afternoon more than a year ago play out in rapid fire bits of memory. Like a video on fast forward I see our big bulky four-wheel-drive suburban spinning out on the highway so we face the wrong way against the oncoming traffic. I see the eighteen-wheeler barreling directly for us. Boris, the Russian goon who is behind the wheel of the Suburban, guns the engine, heads directly for the semi, like he wants to enter into a lethal game of chicken. Only he isn't playing chicken. His thigh is shot through and his leg is paralyzed, his right foot stubbornly bearing down on the gas pedal. Boris turns the wheel to the right, but the operator of the truck turns his wheel to the left. Boris goes left, the truck goes right. Lola is in the back seat. I scream for her to get down. Get down now...

Then the collision...

When the dust settles, I remember falling to my knees on the pavement, holding Lola in my arms. She isn't breathing. There's a tear of blood falling from her left eye. It runs down her cheeks and it touches my hand. My heart is ripped out of me then, because I know she's gone. I gently set her back down onto the road, get up, and walk away. Never once do I look back.

I drink some more beer, wipe my mouth with the back of my trembling hand.

"Newburgh. What did they tell you?"

"Lola Ross was delivered to their emergency room in a state of near death. She suffered internal hemorrhaging from the crash. She died once while en route, was resuscitated and died once on the table and, again, was successfully resuscitated and later on stabilized but critical. She remained in a coma for nearly a month."

"Why didn't someone call me?"

"She had no ID on her when she was delivered to the hospital. The only people with her were the now dead Russians who had kidnapped her. She'd been living in Europe for the past year. She was a blank on the identification radar."

"But when she woke up, Georgie, she would have asked for me."

He shakes his head, drinks down what's left of his

beer, holds the bottle up so Tess can see he needs another.

"Bring a new one for Moon, Tess," he says. "And that shot of Jack."

"Sure about that, Georgie?" she smiles, grabbing the beers from the cooler.

"I'll assume responsibility," he insists.

She sets the new beers in front of us, even though I haven't yet finished my first. Then she pours a hefty shot of Jack, sets that before me. She also pours one for Georgie, sets it beside his new beer.

"Those are on the house, boys," she nods.

"Thank you, beautiful," I say.

She blows me a kiss and shifts back down to the other end of the bar.

"So tell me, Georgie," I say after a beat. "Why didn't she ask for me?"

"It's her memory, Moon. She can't remember much of what happened in her life prior to the accident."

"Total amnesia."

"No," he says, shaking his head. "It's not that simple. She knows who she is, where she comes from, what she does for a living. Only what she can't seem to recall is a block of years. More than likely, the blunt force of the accident resulted in Lola experiencing a traumatic brain injury."

"She's brain damaged?"

"From what I understand, not permanently. I did a little more snooping and found out she's to undergo surgery at the Albany Medical Center on the hippocampus portion of her brain to relieve pressure on the grey matter cortical being caused by scar tissue. If the operation is successful, it's very possible her entire memory will come back to her. A block of years that are presently a big blank will be refilled with memory."

"What years?"

"The years she spent with you, or I can only assume. Be thankful for new developments in brain surgery. Used to be once a brain was damaged and scar tissue formed, nothing could be done. But now, nanotechnology is making it possible for brains to undergo delicate procedures never before attempted or even thought possible." He drinks some beer, wipes his mouth. "You should really think about looking into it yourself. It's possible the bullet planted inside your own brain is ready to be removed."

"Too bad Schroder turned out to be such an asshole. He might have been the surgeon to remove it. For free."

"There's far better surgeons out there. Ones who aren't involved with the Russian mob."

I drink the rest of my first beer, start on the second.

"Is Lola here in Albany?"

"She's here, Moon. Your instincts were right. The woman you saw walking into the coffee shop must have been her."

My insides feel like they're going to rip out of my stomach and spill all over the floor.

"Do you have an address?"

"Now, Moon, you are in no condition to go knocking on her door."

"Why?"

"Because she won't recognize you. You'll scare her off."

"I'll be the judge of that, Georgie," I bark.

"Boys," Tess scolds. "Let's all get along."

"Listen," I say, "if I promise not to go there right away...like this, after I've been drinking...will you give me the address?"

He nods.

"I will give you the address. Under two conditions."

"I'm listening."

"That I don't reveal the address until you're ready,

and I accompany you."

"Any room for bargaining?"

"You've known me almost your whole life."

"Good answer."

He raises up his Jack.

I raise mine up.

"What do we drink to?" I say.

"Lola's alive," he says. "Here's to you getting your shit together, and making her fall in love with you all over again."

Chapter 60

Georgie and I stay at McGeary's for one more shot. Then I tell him it's time I head back home to sober up for young Schroder's birthday party. It's exactly what I do. I head home, undress, slip under the covers. As usual, I make a last check on my phone for any emails I might have missed during the day.

There's a message from Nick Miller.

"These aren't pretty," reads an email accompanied by four photo attachments. "Forensics have concluded that, without a doubt, Amanda committed suicide and she did so with no one else present in the basement of the Senator's house."

I open the email, download the photos.

The first one sends a frigid chill up and down my spine, and most definitely sobers me up.

It's Amanda Bates. She's lying naked on what must be Stephen's bed. She's either passed out, or close to it. A red and black sock is stuffed in her mouth. He's placed his smiling self in the photo, having snapped it as a selfie with his cell phone. In the second photo, he's got her turned over onto her belly and he's straddling her bottom with his pants pulled down around his ankles. Again, he's taken the picture as a selfie, and he's smiling bright eyed for the camera. He makes me want to punch something.

The last two photos, which must have been attached to the email as an afterthought, are the most heartbreaking. Snapped by the APD forensics team, they show a beautiful young woman hanging from a basement rafter, a man's black leather belt around her neck. In each of the photos, her brown eyes are wide open, and her hair is veiling her pale white face.

I slap the phone down on the bed and wonder how it will be possible to sleep when I hate the world so much. But somehow, I manage to drift away.

I wake to the sound of my phone ringing. It's Schroder.

"We have a deal, Moonlight," says the brain surgeon.

"Seven thousand?" I say.

"No," he says. "Ten grand. No negotiation."

"I'll try and get it."

"Bring it with you tonight or no deal."

"I'll do it. I'll be there as soon as I can."

"Oh, and one more thing."

"What is it?"

"In order to seal the deal on our double secret arrangement, I'll need you to prove your allegiance to both me *and* the cause."

The cause...

"Refresh my memory, Doc," I say, knowing precisely what he wants.

"I've already explained my dissatisfaction with those two Russians."

"How could I forget?"

"I'm so glad we can communicate on such a superior level of intelligence, Bruce."

"Me, too, Doc," I say, lifting up my free hand, the middle finger raised high.

"But don't fret," he goes on. "I have a plan. Listen up for the deets..."

Chapter 61

His stupid plan goes something like this: the Russians have not only been invited to his party, they are there already, partying like wild animals. At some point during the festivities, when they're both so liquored and Oxy'd up they can't stand, he wants me to lure them out back to the pool to do some night swimming. Then, when they're in the water, he wants me to shoot them. He'll then have the bodies disposed of and the pool drained.

"You can doooo eeet, Bruce," he says. "Like fish in a barrel." Then he hangs up.

I glance outside. It's dark out. I flick on the light.

Elvis's gear is still laid out on the table. But he's nowhere to be found. That's when I hear someone fumbling around with the front door. My .38 is resting on the counter beside the spy equipment. I slip it out of the shoulder holster, plant a bead on the big slider door as it opens wide and in steps a man.

It's Elvis.

"Jesus, Moon," he says, through heavy breaths. "Expecting company?"

I lower the pistol, stuff it back into the holster on the counter.

"Just a little jumpy," I say. "It's official. The doc wants me to kill the Russians." Then, noticing his gray sweat pants, hooded sweatshirt and Converse high-top sneakers. "Don't tell me you were getting some exercise. Not you, Elvis."

"Hey, the King was all about physical fitness."

"The King was fat."

He closes the door behind him, steps into the loft.

"Popular misconception about the great one. It wasn't for lack of exercise he was so rotund at the end. It was the pain medication he was ingesting for his many physical and mental ailments."

"I'm sure The Beatles gave him a real headache," I say. Then, looking at my watch. "Shower up. We're leaving for the Schroders in ten minutes. You got your Fat Elvis costume...excuse me...you have your Pain-Medicated-Elvis costume ready?"

"Yes, sir."

"You got nine and a half minutes to get ready and gather up your spy gear."

"I only need five," he says, heading for the shower.

While Elvis is cleaning up, I take my .38 back out, thumb the clip release to check the load. The clip is full. In the drawer of the nightstand, I find two more fully loaded clips and place them beside the pistol on the counter. Once more I pull the .22 from my coat pocket, recheck the chambers. The .22 is fully loaded. I return it to the interior coat pocket.

Elvis comes out of the shower with a towel wrapped around him. Rather than go through the pain of watching him force his body into a skin-tight white jumper, I tell him I'll wait for him out in the car.

Five minutes later, Elvis shoots out the door, his thick black hair slicked up in a ducktail doo, the collar on his jumper sky high and that WWE belt wrapped around his gut. For shoes, he's got black high heels. Thick, aluminum framed sunglasses cover his eyes even though it's night time. He's got the equipment, including my .38, stuffed inside a backpack slung over his shoulder. Opening the passenger side door, he tosses the equipment into the back where it falls beside the bag of marked bills.

He gives me a look with that trembling upper lip.

"Let's ride, cowboy," he says, shooting me with the pretend pistol he makes with his right hand.

I turn the key and the engine comes to life. Without a word, I head away from the port.

We drive through the city and then into the suburbs. There's no traffic at night and by eight o'clock we've arrived in Schroder's neighborhood. Even from a few hundred feet away I can see the driveway is empty.

"Thought this was supposed to be a party?" Elvis says.

"A very private party."

"Pull over here," Elvis says, cocking his head over his left shoulder.

I stop the car a few houses up from Schroders.

"This is as far as I go," he says, reaching into the back, grabbing hold of his backpack. "I'll cut through those woods and make my way across to the back of Schroder's house by way of the golf course. I should be able to get a clear shot for the video camera from that position. Sound reception should be great, too. That is, you get him outside on the deck."

"Don't get grass stains on your jumper," I say.

He peers down over his belly at his bell bottoms.

"Thanks for that," he says, genuinely concerned. "Grass stains never come out."

He disappears into the night and through the woods. That's when I reach back into my coat pocket, remove the .22, and stuff it under the driver's seat, easy access. Knowing I freely enter back into hell, I complete the drive to Schroder's house, enter the driveway.

Chapter 62

Anxiety washes over me like someone dumped a bucket of cold blood on my head. I park directly behind the Russian's Caddy. The old boat of a car is beyond conspicuous in the high-end neighborhood. I can only assume the Russians don't know the police are looking for them. Or maybe they just don't care. Probably the latter.

I kill the engine, get out.

From where I'm standing, it looks like every single light in the house has been turned on. The exterior flood lights mounted to the back of the house are lighting up the backyard like a Monday night Yankee's baseball game. I can hear music going. Loud death metal. Guitars grinding, double bass drum thudding, voices grunting and howling. Death dirge. Calling it music is too kind an adjective.

Making my way around back, I spot Schroder. His back is to me. From where I'm standing, the glare from the bright white flood lighting is making it impossible for me to clearly see the person he's talking to. But what I can see is that the brain surgeon is wearing black Gucci loafers, the kind with a silver buckle attached to the front and that cost more cash than my entire collection of jeans, boots, and work-shirts. He's also wearing bright red Bermuda shorts with green whales printed on them. For a shirt, a pink IZOD. I can't see the little alligator that's no doubt stitched to the front over his left man boob, but I'm certain it's there. He's holding a cocktail in his hand and he's spewing forth about something to the invisible man.

The music gets louder. I can almost feel the heavy pounding bass as much as I can hear it. I also make out some laughing and shouting. Shouting coming from the Russians. Hector and Vadim.

I decide to take another couple of steps forward, make my presence known.

"Looks like you have another guest," the invisible man says, in a voice not entirely unfamiliar.

Schroder turns, peers at me.

"Bruce Willis," he says in his happy voice while descending the single step down off the deck. "What a pleasant surprise."

"I was invited, remember?"

"Yes, yes, you were."

He comes up to me, wraps an arm around me, hugs me.

"The Russians are inside getting positively blotto," he whispers into my ear. "When I give the word, I want to you to take them out back. Then you have my blessing to do what you have to do."

"I'm not packing a weapon," I say into his ear, picturing the .22 I stuffed under the driver's seat of the hearse. "Didn't think you'd want me to bring one since it might pose a threat to you and Stephen, considering the, ummm, up and down nature of our relationship. But I did bring your money. Ten Gs."

He takes a moment to pat me down, up and down one thigh, and up and down the other. He seems to enjoy the process.

"You're a smart man, Moonlight," he says. "Maybe you assumed if you didn't bring a gun, you wouldn't have to perform your sacred duty, which is none other than ridding my life of those wretched Russians." He pats my left facial cheek with a loose open hand. "But guess what. I've got you covered. I own one of several pistols you may use." Then, planting that pumpkin head smile on his face that I've come to hate. "Now allow me to introduce you to one of your new business partners."

I feel my heart sink, knowing I might have to kill Hector and Vadim after all.

"Partners?" I say. "Thought we were working alone."

"Not on your life. There's mucho dinero to be made in the Oxy smuggling business. I have many partners. In fact, you'd be surprised how deeply my network runs."

"Indeed I would," I say.

He takes hold of my hand, like I'm his new bitch. I feel his sweaty palm and soft, chubby hand in mine and it makes my stomach turn. He leads me around to the deck so that, for the first time since I arrived on the scene, the floodlights are no longer blinding and the invisible man becomes plainly visible. Now it makes sense why his voice sounded so familiar. I know this man. We were recently introduced.

It's the late Amanda Bates' father.

The Honorable Senator Jeffery Bates.

Chapter 63

"Can't say I expected to see you here, Senator," I say. "In fact, I should think this is the last place you'd want to be."

He holds out his hand for me. I have no choice but to shake it. It's a thinner hand than Schroder's. But somehow just as soft, dead, cold, and wet.

"Oh well, there's the public me," he says, pursing his lips together. "And then there's the private me who misses his daughter terribly, but who recognizes a great business venture when it stares him in the face."

"Pushing Oxy."

"Oxy is a pharmaceutical. It's not like we're dealing in heroin or crack cocaine to the minorities of the world."

He's giving me this look like he's not really believing his own words, which shouldn't be a stretch for him, considering his role as a professional politician. But the way he's blinking rapidly, licking his lips and gums, and sniffling hard through his nostrils tells me something else: it tells me the good Senator isn't into selling Oxy for money he probably doesn't need, but instead he's being coerced into pushing it by the very man who facilitates his drug habit. That man being Doc Schroder.

"Never truer words have been spoken," I say, praying Elvis is getting this with his audio-visual setup. "Oxy is practically an over-the-counter drug. Where's the harm in selling a little on the side, Senator? It's like a hobby."

Schroder joins us and the music gets louder the closer

216

I come to the house.

"Do you have the money, Moonlight?"

"In the car. Shall I retrieve it?"

He holds up his hand.

"No, not quite yet." Shooting me a wink. "After you finish your first order of business." He turns, puts his hand on the sliding glass door. "Gentlemen, perhaps now is a good time to sing Happy Birthday to my dear son, Stephen."

I follow both men inside.

The death metal is deafening. The kitchen is a covered in empty beer cans and vodka bottles. Dozens of Oxy capsules occupy the surface of the big kitchen table to my left, along with two good sized mirrors, lines of coke laid out on them. Instead of passing right by the table and into the living room, Schroder stops at it, bends over and, using a rolled up dollar bill like a short straw, he shoves into his nostril, snorts a line the size of my index finger. Setting the rolled up bill back onto the mirror, he places his index finger in a glass that's still got some vodka in it. He sets the vodka-soaked finger under his nostril and inhales the liquid. Then he clothespins his nose and breathes in even harder so the coke he just inhaled rushes into his brain. As a final gesture, he presses the index finger onto some of the coke and rubs it over his gums.

"Wooo wooo," he shouts, "That's some damn good shit, Senator."

That's when I hear the sound of a toilet flushing. A door opens up behind me and a woman steps out of the bathroom. It's Lisa, Bates' sister-in-law. She's dressed in a red mini-dress with matching suit jacket, along with black stockings and leather pumps. Her dark hair is parted over her left eye, just like Lola would do, and she glares at me wide-eyed.

"Oh," she says. "It's you."

"Welcome to the party," I say. "Or maybe you should be saying that to me."

She steps out and nearly trips over her own feet. I manage to catch her before she falls.

"Oh my," she says, slurring her words. "A little too much to drink."

"And snort," I say.

Letting go of her, I take a look over my left shoulder. I see the business-suited senator staring down at one of the mirrors filled with glorious white nose powder.

"Don't mind if I do," he says, repeating Schroder's coke inhalation process movement for movement. "There, now that makes me feel a whole lot better. Like I can take on the entire world. Like I can be, dare I say it, President of the United States of America."

He steps on over to me, hands me the rolled up bill. I look at Lisa, and she looks at me. Without having to say a word, I know what she's thinking: you don't tell anyone about our impromptu fuck session inside your loft, I won't tell anyone you're working for the cops.

"How's about it, Moonlight?" the Senator says. "You don't look like a stranger to snow in May."

I take the bill in hand.

A soldier's got to do what a soldier's got to do.

I bend down over the mirror, sniff up a line. The effect is immediate. My damaged brain suddenly feels like it's healed again, my synapses on fire. I rub a dab of the coke on my gums and feel the pleasant numbness settle in. Suddenly the thought of having to kill two Russian thugs doesn't seem so bad. But then, maybe it won't come to that. Maybe if Elvis has collected enough evidence with his spy gear to convict these clowns, I can call in Miller's cavalry earlier than expected and end this party, pronto.

"Please grab a beverage, gentleman," Schroder insists, as he freshens up his drink with a full bar that's been set up on the kitchen counter. "Beer's in the fridge."

I go to the refrigerator. As promised, it's stocked with beer. I grab one, pop the tab, take a deep drink. I have to admit, Schroder knows how to party. But then, I already knew that. Drinks in hand, the four of us then proceed into the living room. The music is blaring through an iPod system of Bose speakers that boast a big volume punch. Stephen is seated on the couch, passing in and out of consciousness, a big glob of vomit staining his baby blue IZOD, and a piss stain soaking his white Bermuda shorts. The site of him is enough to sober me up and remember why I'm here.

The two Russians are dancing to the music, glasses of vodka in hand, lit cigarettes planted in their mouths. They're wearing the same tracksuits they always wear, their black hair slicked back against their cannon ball heads.

"Look what dog dragged in," Hector, says in his deeply accented voice. "It's Dickbreath Moonlight, da?" Then, smiling. "Get it? Dick...Breath?"

Vadim stops dancing, looks Hector up and down.

"It's 'Look what cat dragged in' stupid fucking big dumb moron," he spits. "Not dog."

Hector stops dancing.

"Dogs I like better than cats," he says. "The cats, they make me sneeze, da?"

Schroder goes to the iPod, pulls it from the dock, presses Stop.

"Everyone gather around," he announces. "I'd like to sing happy birthday to my one and only pride and joy. My son, Stephen."

"But wait!" Vadim shouts. "You have no cake?"

We stare down at Stephen. Head bobbing, mumbling

something indiscernible, he's oblivious to us.

"Who needs cake to sing Happy Birthday?" the Doc says.

"Exactly," the Senator says. "Let's just sing and enjoy the festivities." He raises up his glass, clears his throat. *"Happy birthday to you..."* he begins to sing.

"Wait, wait, Senator Drug Addict," Vadim insists, waving his hands in the air. "Hector, go get surprise."

Hector turns, heads back out into the kitchen. Within seconds, I can make out the sound of him rummaging around inside some cabinets and then opening and closing the oven door, like maybe he's hidden something inside it. And maybe he has, because when he comes back in, he's carrying a big sheet cake. There's a bunch of candles on it, and they're lit. He carries the cake over to Stephen. The cake is both thick and big, and beneath the candles is an image of Al Pacino as *Scarface*. *Scarface* is made out of different colored frostings, but the image is uncanny. The master froster, whoever he or she is, nailed precisely Pacino's white leisure suit, cropped black hair, and even the scowl on his scarred face.

"Oh my, Stephen seems just a little too drunk to work up a big bunch of air, Hector," the Doc says. "Maybe I should blow the candles out for him."

"No, no," Vadim says. "That would be bad luck." Then, turning back to Hector. "You know what to do, big fella."

Once more Hector disappears into the kitchen. This time when he returns, he's holding one of the mirrors filled with a small hill of cocaine in one hand, and in the other, he's holding a small video camera. Placing the mirror under Stephen's nose, Vadim tells the kid to inhale.

"Do like *Scarface*, Stephen," Hector insists, the video camera now poised at eye level. "You must say, 'My wife, she can't have a leetle baby.' Say that...say the line, da?"

Stephen drops his face into the hill of cocaine, inhales. When he lifts his face up, the entire bottom half is covered in white powder.

"Say it...say it," Hector pushes like the director of a big budget Hollywood epic. "Say *Scarface* thing."

"My baby," Stephen drunkenly mumbles, "she can't even haff a leetle wife."

Lisa lets out a high pitched laugh and nearly falls flat on her face while going for the couch. She somehow manages to keep her balance before collapsing onto the cushions, her head resting only a few inches away from Stephen's right thigh.

"No," Hector says, jerking the video camera from his face. "It's 'My wife, she can't even haff a leetle baby!' Stupid fucking brat boy."

"Easy, Hector," Schroder smiles, "that's my son and your boss you're speaking to."

"Blow out candles, Stephen," Vadim insists, trying to avoid what is fast becoming a train wreck.

"He's not my boss," Hector says working up a wad of mucous, spitting it onto the floor. "I have no boss."

"Hector, please," Senator Bates barks, his face taking on a green hue as he stares down at the wad of yellow, blood-laced goop.

"Come Stephen," Vadim presses, placing the lit candles directly below the kid's mouth. "Blow!"

Stephen inhales a deep breath, puckers his lips, and lets loose with a rush of air.

The candles don't blow out.

"Trick candles," Doc Schroder says. "Oh, how fun."

Stephen inhales again, let's loose with another, harder breath.

That's when Vadim turns his head, drops the cake into Stephen's lap, shouting, "Fire in the hole!"

Chapter 64

What follows is not one explosion, but three separate explosions. Or, more specifically, ear piercing short, sharp cracks that sound like a high caliber rifle discharging high capacity rounds. I hit the floor. So does the Senator and the brain surgeon.

"Oh God! Oh God!" shouts the politician. "I think I'm hit."

His chest is covered in frosting.

"Am I dead?" Schroder cries.

Meanwhile, the Russians are bent over in laughter.

"Exploding cake!" Vadim shouts. "Filled with M80s. Old Soviet army birthday surprise! It's no fun unless someone lose a finger or two, da?"

I wipe away frosting from my face with the back of my hand, stand up. Stephen is covered in cake and frosting.

Beside him on the couch, is Lisa. She's not moving. There's something dripping from her left eye socket. It's blood and the eyeball is missing. Obviously M80s weren't the only deadly thing stored inside the surprise Soviet army cake.

"It is big ass gag," Vadim says through a shit-eating smile. "Like in your television program, *Five Stooges*."

"*Three Stooges*, stupid fuck," Hector corrects. He's still videotaping like the exploding cake is all a part of his script.

"Whatever," Vadim says. "No harm done, da?"

"No harm?" shouts the Senator. "No fucking harm? You've killed Lisa."

The politician goes to her, kneels down on the floor, shakes Lisa. She's not responding.

"She's dead!" he cries.

"Hey, Hector," Vadim says, "this isn't Soviet barracks. You were supposed to leave the screw-and-nail shrapnel out of the cake."

"Oops," Hector smiles. "I forget Obama Americans don't like to play rough no more."

Stephen, awake now, shoots a glare at Hector my long dead dad can feel. Without even attempting to wipe his face off, he reaches around the small of his back, comes back out with a chrome-plated automatic.

"Stephen, put that down!" Schroder insists.

"Shut up, old man," the suddenly sobered up and very angry kid says while slowly rising up from the couch. "You want *Scarface*, you Russian fucks. Well then 'Say Hello to my leetle fuckin' frien...'" He cocks back the hammer. Fires. The piece of wall directly above Vadim explodes. The Russian goon reaches into his sweatsuit jacket, frees his own automatic. Hector joins him with his .44 Magnum. The two Russians and Stephen are pointing the barrels of their respective hand cannons in one another's frosting spattered faces.

Then something unexpected happens. The front door opens.

"Well it's one for the money!" a voice sings out. *"Two for the show! Three to get ready, now go cat go!"*

All heads turn.

"It's Elvis!" Hector shouts. "Elvis fucking Presley."

"Dead Elvis in flesh!" Vadim shouts.

"I hate Elvis," Stephen barks.

Elvis takes on the pose of a black belt karate man, reaches under his cape, grabs hold of my .38, tosses it to me. I catch it, drop to the floor, let loose with a spray of rounds that makes the Russians dive for cover.

I see Stephen's gun. It's pointed at me. I point mine at

him, squeeze off another round. It doesn't connect with his chubby flesh and bone, but instead nails the portion of V-shaped couch cushion in between his thighs. He screams like a girl. The Senator bounds up from a crouch, tries to run away, but Elvis gives chase, dives, tackles him at the ankles.

Catching a quick glimpse of Schroder coming at me, I raise myself up onto one knee.

I look up.

That's when I see a black ceramic ashtray come down on my forehead.

Chapter 65

When I come to, my head feels like it's been split down the center and sewed back up with fishing line. Soon as I can focus my eyes, I see we've been packed into the master bath off the doc's bedroom. Elvis, the Senator, Schroder, and I are duct-taped to kitchen chairs, hands taped behind our backs at the wrists, tape covering our mouths. Our chairs have been positioned in front of a stand-alone bathtub that can fit up to four people. Directly before us is a window wall looking out onto a small wood of tall trees lit up in spotlight and, beyond that, the country club golf course bathed in darkness. The Senator is to my left. Elvis is to my right. To his right sits Schroder. The heavy metal is once more blaring downstairs where the body of Lisa is likely still lying on the couch, bleeding out, thanks to an exploding cake filled with metal screws.

Stephen has not been duct-taped to a chair.

He's standing directly behind his father. He's got a gas-powered chainsaw clutched in his hands. Behind him, Hector has his .44 Magnum pressed up against the kid's head.

"Start saw, Stephen," Hector directs. "As you hold saw, you say '*Antonio, watch what happens to your friend. You don't want this to happen to you.*' You got it, da?"

Vadim is standing off to the side. This time, he's in charge of filming. The video camera pressed to his grinning face, he's recording everything going down in the bathroom. The satchel containing Miller's ten grand is on the floor by his sneakered feet, the zipper opened. I can only wonder if he spotted my .22 stuffed under the driver's seat when he retrieved the bag of cash. It also makes me wonder if he knew what Doc Schroder was planning for him and his partner all along. My gut tells me he did.

"Ready, set, action!" Vadim shouts.

Stephen awkwardly pulls the ripcord on the chainsaw. Unluckily for him, it starts up on the first tug, the buzzing deafeningly loud, exhaust spitting out bits of flame and smoke like a man-eating dragon. Stephen is revving the motor and crying so hard he can barely stand. Like Steven Spielberg's evil twin brother, Hector reaches out with his hand, points at the exact place he wants the kid to begin cutting his father's right arm off.

The brain surgeon starts to squirm. He's panicking and screaming through the duct tape.

"Say line, da?" Hector says. "You know line. You watch the *Scarface* one-thousand times before, da? You watch with me, with Vadim. You replay chainsaw scene, many more times."

The chainsaw is bobbing in Stephen's hands. He looks like he's about to pass out from fear and from the booze, Oxy, and coke floating through his veins. If he drops the saw, it will take his foot off.

"The line," Hector insists. "Say line."

Stephen opens his mouth, just enough to speak through the strands of snot pouring out of his nose. "Antonio...watch what happens...to your friend...You don't want...this to happen...to you."

"Da, da!" shouts Hector. "Now cut it off!"

Stephen lets loose with a burst of new tears as the screaming buzzsaw blade enters into his father's arm, spraying the entire room with blood, bone, and pieces of pink flesh.

The arm drops to the floor with a thud.

A now in-shock Doc Schroder is rocking back and forth in his chair while Elvis passes out, chin against barrel chest. Some of the blood spatter has sprayed onto his white Elvis jumpsuit. He'll never get the stains out now. Not even if he Shout's it out. Doc Schroder is squirming in his chair, yelping something high-pitched and heart wrenching. The nub of flesh where his arm used to be is twitching while blood pumps out of it like an open spigot.

Stephen is hysterical, his face, arms and chest covered in a thin layer of dark arterial blood.

Vadim is happy as a clam and it shows on his red-speckled face.

"You know next line," an excited Hector insists. "You know what to do."

Stephen holds up the saw once more, positions it over his father's right leg.

"Now...the leg...huh?"

The saw revs once more. Stephen takes aim while his father desperately tries to get away but can't possibly move due to the binding duct tape. The red laser that flashes through the picture window doesn't register at first. And even if it did, there's not a damn thing any of us can do about it. Especially Stephen who, at present, is oblivious to everything that's happening around him, except for the pit of despair he's drowning in. But the despair is over in the flash of a rifle burst as a bullet makes a round hole in the glass window and then enters his forehead, making jelly filling of his brains before exiting sloppily out the back.

Vadim is still shooting with the video camera.

Hector stands there, a dumb looking expression occupying his square face as he turns to the window, catches his own red laser beam and his own bullet. He hasn't yet dropped to the floor before Vadim's head explodes like a water balloon filled with red dye no. 2.

Then it's Doctor Schroder's turn, as the squirming, suffering brain surgeon falls peacefully still, what's left of his own brain spilling down the front of his IZOD.

I can't say I'm afraid as the laser shoots and scoots all around the room, at one point planting a bead on the Senator's forehead, but then quickly disappearing without once having landed on myself or Elvis. Maybe it's the effects of the cocaine I snorted earlier. Or the fact the Russians and the Schroders are now decidedly dead and we're tied up. Maybe it's simply because the heavy metal death rock has stopped playing. But despite the carnage of the evening, I'm thinking clearly.

Case and point: I know whoever did the shooting was most definitely not the cops. Definitely not SWAT. Definitely not the local Sheriff. Law enforcement doesn't act that way. They would, in essence, announce their presence like the mounted cavalry blowing their trumpets.

Whoever did the shooting knew precisely who to kill and who not to kill. I'm just thankful I'm not the one who had to do the killing.

I turn my head, glance at Elvis as he wakes up. He's lost his sunglasses and his eyes are open wide and filled with as much fear as they were before he passed out. Despite the DNA that stains it, his grease-filled hair is perfect. I try and get my hands and my ankles free. But the duct tape is too tight. Too binding. We're stuck here until someone finds us.

Just me, Elvis, a State Senator, the dead Schroders, and a couple of Hollywood-obsessed drug runners whose souls can't get through the gates of hell fast enough.

Chapter 66

Then comes a wonderful sight. No more than three minutes later, the glare of red, white, and blue halogen lights flash through the bullet-riddled window glass. It combines with a wonderful sound. Sirens blaring. From where Elvis and I are sitting, it sounds like an army of policemen and women. For once, I will be so glad to see them.

Another half minute passes before I make out the sounds of lug soles pounding up the staircase. Full combat/riot gear-wearing police officers burst into the bathroom, spraying the dark room with a half dozen red laser sights that flicker on and off the walls like a light show at a cheesy Moscow discotheque.

"Moonlight!" I hear, coming from one of the cops behind me. "You alive?"

I try and mumble a feeble "Yes" through my duct tape. But I'm not sure Detective Miller can make out what I'm saying.

He comes around front, rips off the tape.

"You ripped my lips off!" I bark.

He smiles.

"Oops," he says. Then, looking down at the dead bodies, including one severed arm, "What the fuck happened here?"

"We had a little birthday party," I say. "Didn't go so well toward the end."

Miller looks at Elvis, then turns and stares at the Senator.

"They okay?"

"Yup," I say as the cops begin to undo our tape. "But you might want to trade the senator's duct tape for a pair of handcuffs. He and the late Doctor Schroder were partners in the Oxy selling operation. The doc was into it for the cashish, but the senator was into it for the hashish. We have the evidence on tape. Oh, and you'll find his deceased dead sister-in-law downstairs on the couch. Her reasons for getting mixed up in this are probably a combination of easy money and drugs, plus all the sex she could pile high on her dinner plate."

"Someone shoot her in the eye?"

"No, she died by trick exploding Soviet army birthday cake...don't ask."

One of the cops frees Elvis.

He stands.

"This PI shit ain't fun no more," he says. "I quit, Moonlight. Are we square now?"

"You can go, Elvis. Your work is done here. And yes, we are square."

He goes to leave.

"Ahh, Elvis," Miller says. "Don't go far. I'll need a statement from you later."

"I need a drink," he says. I can hear him bounding down the stairs.

Finally, I'm freed. I stand, rubbing my wrists. My eyes are planted on the politician who is still duct-taped to the kitchen chair. The cops are obviously in no hurry to free him.

"There goes the career, Senator," I say.

He silently stares back at me like he's disappointed that he continues to breathe. Knowing how bad it's going to be when the media and the voting public burn him alive, I can't say I blame him.

Outside on the front lawn, I light a cigarette while an

EMT van drives up onto the grass, as well as two long, black Chevy Suburbans with tinted windows. The EMT van is for the Senator, but the Suburbans are for carrying away the dead. Trust the son of a mortician, they've got their work cut out for them.

Miller issues a series of orders to the dozen or more cops holding court on the front lawn, the chatter from the radios on the six or seven lit up cruisers surrounding the place filling the air. The tinny chatter sounds somehow better than the death metal I've had to suffer tonight. He makes his way through the cops and through a growing crowd of reporters and neighborhood sightseers who are only now beginning to gather like flies on shit.

"Let's take a walk, Deputy," he orders.

"You're the boss," I say, following him into the darkness around the backside of the house.

We walk to the far perimeter of the property to the tree line.

"We picked up Kevin Woods on foot as he was crossing over the golf course," Miller explains. "When some neighbors called in saying they heard what sounded like gunshots coming from Schroder's property, we came running."

"I warned you about Kevin," I say. "He had his laser sights set on the Schroders a long time ago. All he needed was something like what happened to Amanda to work up his courage to finally do it."

Miller reaches into his pocket, takes out a mini-Maglite, fingered the Latex covered switch, shines the bright circle of light onto the ground. Resting on top of the leaves are four brass shell casings.

"Looks like thirty-aught-six," he says. "Must have been perched up in this old oak. Gave him a perfect,

231

unobstructed line of fire into the bathroom. Probably wouldn't even need a scope at this range if he were doing his killing during the daylight hours."

"He used a laser sight. Probably an infrared scope, too."

"Really?" Miller says, as if surprised. "Good for him."

I catch the smile that forms on his face as he turns his flashlight off.

"He'll get a fair trial," he adds. "As for the Senator, my guess is Kevin wanted to leave him alive in order to make him face the inevitable shame and humiliation. Perfect. Exactly what I would have done."

I can't exactly see him, but I know his smile has grown even wider.

"You knew, didn't you," I say. "You knew Kevin was going to strike tonight."

"I didn't know for sure. One can never be certain of such things. Like they say, revenge is a dish better served cold." He pauses to breathe in and out. "But I had a hunch that cold dish just might get served up tonight. A good, solid hunch."

I smoke my cigarette, exhale some blue smoke against the night sky.

"It's not right," I say. "Maybe not the Russians, but even the Schroders had their right to a fair trial."

"Maybe," he says, taking a step or too back toward the house. "But it would have been expensive. And, who knows, in the end, a soulless lawyer might have found a way to get both those creeps off. On a technicality or something. I've seen it happen before."

"Do their deaths pay for Amanda's death?"

"I think so."

"Do they wipe away the memory of your wife's death?"

He looks up at the sky, as if proceeding to ask his

wife that very question. After a time, he nods and whispers, "You, too, babe? If you're good with it, then I'm good with it." Then, lowering his head, he turns back to me.

"Nothing will ever erase the memory of her death. But at least now we both feel as though we can live with it."

For a brief but heavy moment, we stand in silence, while my cigarette burns down to my fingertips.

"We done here, Moonlight?"

"You tell me. I'm your official deputy bitch these days."

"Ex-deputy bitch," he says. "Job well done."

I reach into my coat pocket, grab the temporary badge and hand it over. He stuffs it into his jacket pocket and walks away, his rangy body fading back into the darkness of this long, long night.

Me? I flick what's left of the burning cig into the woods. I would not be sad if this house burned down. Turning up the collar on my leather coat, I take my time returning to the scene, whistling, "We're caught in a trap..." the entire way.

Epilogue

It's another three days before I'm ready for Georgie to pick me up in his pickup truck.

When I get in I can hardly feel my legs, as I close the door, strap on my seatbelt.

"You ready for this, Moonlight?" he says, his blue eyes hidden behind a pair of Ray-Ban sunglasses, his long hair still in a ponytail.

"No," I say. Then, "Yes."

"When was the last time you had a drink?"

"Three days ago."

"Promise?"

"Scout's honor."

Driving away from the loft, he makes his way across the abandoned parking lot all the way to Broadway, where he hooks a right. We drive for a while through the city until we come to the northern edge of town in an area that formerly housed the steel mills, lumber yards, and warehouses, but that now has become rehabilitated and gentrified into apartments and lofts for young urban professionals and artists.

He pulls up to a five-story brick structure that's been painted white.

"Her number is 5B," he says. "She'll let you in because she's expecting her monthly Fed Ex delivery of meds. Blood thinners, mostly to prevent stroke. You know the score, what with that head of yours."

"I don't know what I'd do without you, Georgie."

"I'm not sure what you would do, either," he says. "As far as Lola goes, she won't be getting her meds right now."

I look down at my hands. They're trembling.

"Right now, she's going to get me instead. Whether she wants me or not."

"She'll learn to want you again, Moon. Just be yourself." He reaches into the back storage area behind the seats, comes back around with some flowers gripped in his hand. A springtime assortment of daisies, orchids, petunias, and some other stuff I don't recognize. "Go get her back, tiger," he adds, handing me the bouquet.

I open the door, slip on out of the truck.

I cross the street, enter into the building's vestibule through the front glass door. I see the buzzer for 5B, the name "Ross" taped above it in black block letters. Well, at least she remembers her name. Inhaling a deep breath that does nothing to slow the pulse pounding in my temples, I press the buzzer.

After a few long seconds, I hear a voice. A voice I recognize. A voice from the dead.

"Yes," she says.

"Delivery," I swallow.

"Come on up."

There's an electronic buzz and then the door opens. I push my way through it, take the elevator to the fifth floor. I walk the brightly lit hall, not feeling the soles of my feet as they strike the linoleum-covered surface. By the time I come to the door marked 5B, I can hardly breathe. It takes almost all of my strength to raise my hand, extend my index finger, press the doorbell.

The buzzer sounds.

I pray to God above I don't make a fool of myself by passing out at her doorstep.

I hear light footsteps, then a hand grabbing hold of the handle, and another hand unlatching the deadbolt. The door opens. I see her face. Lola's beautifully tanned, brown-eyed face, her dark hair tumbling over her shoulders.

"Hello," she says, looking into my eyes. "I've been expecting you."

Moonlight weeps.

Photo Credit: Jessica Painter/Edward Smathers

Vincent Zandri is the NEW YORK TIMES and USA TODAY bestselling author of more than sixteen novels, including THE INNOCENT, GODCHILD, THE REMAINS, MOONLIGHT FALLS, and THE SHROUD KEY. A freelance photo-journalist and traveler, he is also the author of the blog, The Vincent Zandri Vox. He lives in New York and Florence, Italy. For more go to http://www.vincentzandri.com/.

OTHER TITLES FROM DOWN AND OUT BOOKS

See www.DownAndOutBooks.com for complete list

By J.L. Abramo
Catching Water in a Net
Clutching at Straws
Counting to Infinity
Gravesend
Chasing Charlie Chan
Circling the Runway (*)

By Trey R. Barker
2,000 Miles to Open Road
Road Gig: A Novella
Exit Blood

By Richard Barre
The Innocents
Bearing Secrets
Christmas Stories
The Ghosts of Morning
Blackheart Highway
Burning Moon
Echo Bay
Lost

By Rob Brunet
Stinking Rich

By Milton T. Burton
Texas Noir

By Reed Farrel Coleman
The Brooklyn Rules

By Tom Crowley
Vipers Tail
Murder in the Slaughterhouse

By Frank De Blase
Pine Box for a Pin-Up
Busted Valentines and Other Dark Delights
The Cougar's Kiss (*)

By Les Edgerton
The Genuine, Imitation, Plastic Kidnapping

By A.C. Frieden
Tranquility Denied
The Serpent's Game

By Jack Getze
Big Numbers
Big Money
Big Mojo

By Keith Gilman
Bad Habits

By Terry Holland
An Ice Cold Paradise
Chicago Shiver

(*)—Coming Soon

OTHER TITLES FROM DOWN AND OUT BOOKS

See www.DownAndOutBooks.com for complete list

By Darrel James,
Linda O. Johnston &
Tammy Kaehler (editors)
Last Exit to Murder

By David Housewright
& Renée Valois
The Devil and the Diva

By David Housewright
Finders Keepers
Full House

By Jon Jordan
Interrogations

By Jon & Ruth Jordan (editors)
Murder and Mayhem in
Muskego

By Bill Moody
Czechmate
The Man in Red Square
Solo Hand
The Death of a Tenor Man
The Sound of the Trumpet
Bird Lives!

By Gary Phillips
The Perpetrators
Scoundrels (Editor)
Treacherous

By Gary Phillips, Tony Chavira
& Manoel Maglhaes
Beat L.A. (Graphic Novel)

By Robert J. Randisi
Upon My Soul
Souls of the Dead
Envy the Dead (*)

By Lono Waiwaiole
Wiley's Lament
Wiley's Shuffle
Wiley's Refrain
Dark Paradise

By Vincent Zandri
Moonlight Weeps

(*)—Coming Soon

Transit to: SEAST
Transit library: ALPH
Title: Moonlight weeps : a
Moonlight P.I. mystery

FICTION ZANDRI

Zandri, Vincent.
Moonlight weeps

SEAST

R4001723279

SOUTHEAST
Atlanta-Fulton Public Library

CPSIA info
Printed in th
LVOW10s2

451141